Forbidden

A Novella by

Erin Crocker

Edited by
Linette Kasper

Cover Design by
Leslie Safford

Forbidden

Erin Crocker

Copyright © 2018 Erin Crocker

All rights reserved. Except for brief excerpts in reviews, this book may not be reproduced or distributed in any printed or electronic form without the prior express written permission of the author.

This is a work of fiction. Names, characters, places, and incidents either are products of the author's imagination or are used fictitiously. Any resemblance to actual events or locales or persons, living or dead, is entirely coincidental.

ISBN: **978-0-578-44082-8**

Here I am, publishing another novel or novella, rather. I couldn't have done it without the help of Linette a.k.a "Linedits"—author of "Daimon" and "Rogue"—who takes the time to carefully edit all of my manuscripts thus far. Jensen Reed—co-editor-in-chief of Pixie Forest Publishing—who is one friggin' amazing P.A. who pushes me to try new and cool things on social media. And to Leslie Safford who creates the most amazing covers ever!! I would also like to thank my beta readers Charles Reis, Robin Smith, and Rick Pinzon Jr. for their willingness to offer genuine and helpful criticisms, thoughts, and suggestions. Finally, no acknowledgement section is complete without saying something about best friends, Randy, you're one of the best. And a BIG SHOUT OUT to my kids who read this and were upset that I hadn't included them yet in the draft. Hi Kids!

Prologue

"Shall we retreat to the cellar?" Constance Colstock looked to her husband as thunderous knocks persisted against the wooden door of the Paradise Grove parsonage.

"Nay, we shall not. For the will of God is strong for those who terry not in faithlessness." Abel's voice didn't waiver. "Piety." He gestured at the youngest daughter who cowered at her father's voice. "Ready thyself."

The young girl shrugged into the corner next to her older brother as Abel reached for the door. "Abel Colstock," the voice from outside reverberated through the humble parsonage. "Open this door! For we, your townspeople, your church, heard the shrieks of children from the woods." Colstock swallowed hard as Elkanah continued. "Talked, have we, and upon this night, thou shalt render payment for the violations of God's little ones."

Abel's hands didn't shake as he pushed the door open and held his palms to a group of angry citizens. To the side of them were onlookers. Colstock smirked. "Shrieks and wails of little ones, in the woods? Of what dost thou speak, Elkanah?" He motioned to the faction of citizens who stood, ready to destroy him and all that he had built. "To what end has thou brought thine own jury to my home at this hour?" He lowered his brows. "To my family?"

"To the end of evil. To the end of the frightened cries of small children that sound through the deep bark of thick trees that doth reach our ears. To the end that thou must pay. For didst I hear cries with such clarity one night while dipping into the clear creek that doth divide us from the barren land across the way. I must—"

"The payment of sin is through thy death." A lady's impatient shout pierced the crowd. "Thou hast family, dost thou not? For, put to death they shall be, as well."

A few people cried out in agreement.

Abel Colstock's mind spun with vigor. His legacy, the church and community his family struggled to establish, all of it could be gone on that night. He thought. "By and by..." he shushed the crowd. "For this night, this eve of the grand trial before us all hath our God whispered to my ear, for all who will believe, this...this creek that Elkanah, that many members of this group and of this community do go to bathe." He inhaled. Seconds ticked by before he spoke once more. "'Tis possessed by that of the...uh...the..." *God give me words*, he thought to himself. "...Devil."

Upon Colstock's proclamation, everyone took a step back. Elkanah turned to both crowds. "Hear it *not*. Hear not his words. For he hath want to save himself."

"Nay," Colstock countered and wiped a spot of sweat that formed along his hairline. "For disbelief is the key to an ungodly heart. What these people, these executioners doth hear would be the screams of Hell, the cries of those next to whom they shall suffer in hellfire." The pastor's confidence in his own lie grew as he continued, "Bathing in that creek has tainted them. They have a...they have a..." eyes, throughout the group of onlookers, widened. "It's...The Sickness, and I say, upon this unholy night, that they have want to contaminate this Divine Establishment. Yea, though, I shall have mercy. Yes, mercy upon them. For not death, but banishment, banishment shall be their punishment."

One Hundred Years Later

One

Reverend Elijah Colstock tapped his foot to the cadence of pattering rain against the parsonage window. The afternoon found him in a melancholy disposition that even the humid melody of nature failed to remedy.

His ear tingled and he massaged it. *It is time.* The whisper seemed to originate at his hairline. *It is time.*

The nervous man struggled to stand. Once he managed, he leaned his weight against the mahogany desk. "What?" echoed its way through the otherwise empty room. Still balancing against the counter, he shuffled until he stood on the other side, taking significant caution by checking his peripheral. "What do you want?"

Menacing laughter carved a path and spiraled its way into Colstock's bones, digging deep enough to impose a shattered chill that excited the man and forced his shaken body to retreat to his original position of sitting.

Sweat tickled and pooled into the creases of his strained forehead. He rubbed the side of his ear. "Dare you enter the house of God?" he challenged, regaining a sudden sense of power. After all, he'd been ordained by God Himself. It was the Colstock family that had led their people from the tyranny of Towne Greene, but for what more than to escape the gross misinterpretations of the Word, to run from the blasphemy. All were mere memories to Colstock—stories and truths handed down from generations of the family line.

His cough was brief, and he finished by a rough clearing of his throat. The Old Ways would lead his people to Providence, but they could only be sought after in an environment of order and control, not Towne Greene's theatrical kaleidoscope of chaos that spoke of wholeness through expression and creativity. To those who would dare channel their predisposition of the Jezebelian spirit, penance was only solved through the sacrifice of death.

Adultery, lust, all the materialistic sins that came along with The Sickness had been weeded out by his ancestors—his all too gracious and lenient family lineage who, in place of death, rendered a verdict of banishment to the arid land across the tainted creek. That thought prompted an awareness into the reverend that perhaps, it was just that weakness that was the source of his midday chagrin.

His ear popped, and he jumped at the sharp knock that interrupted his thought. "Do, find yourself welcome to enter."

The grating squeal of the door as it opened revealed a young courier, who, in brevity and no more, reminded the man of his childhood self. "Reverend." The boy half-bowed, and Colstock adjusted himself in response. "You sent for post service."

"Ahh, yes." He paused and studied the young boy. "Alas, son, you run the town uncovered during this bout of rain?" Another cough struggled its way out of Colstock's throat. "You'll catch your death."

The boy cocked his head. "Sir?"

"You heard me." He pointed a still-shaking finger at the window. "The rain."

Pieces of stray hairs shook down, and the boy pushed them from his eyes in order to properly follow the point of reference. "The...r-rain? Sir, the sunshine is quite blinding...a-all due r-respect."

Colstock squeezed his eyes shut, hard. Time passed; he focused on the precipitation that pattered against the roof. Harder. He opened them and flinched at the bright glow of light that shone where, just moments before, drops of rain had drummed their way into his awareness. Rapid sweat drizzled down his forehead, causing him to make a quick job of removing his spectacles to clean and adjust them. Time was tedious and silent as it passed.

"S-sir?"

The older man frowned. "Yes." He signed a parchment paper before folding and securing it with the official seal of The Church. His wavering hand extended. "Here, deliver this, with haste, to the Dawning family. You know the way, boy?"

The boy met his question with a nod.

"Then go." Slow, small taps sounded against the oak floor as the child backed up a few steps. "*Go*," Colstock repeated. The boy's eyes widened, and he turned and ran. The reverend grimaced when his sore back met the anthemion design of his wooden chair.

Time—his time, the Lord's time—it neared, when truth and justice would once again be established in Paradise Grove. Perhaps the Dawning's would come to call later that afternoon for a brief plea of their case. He scoffed. The answer, of course, would be no. How could he be expected to subject his Divine people to another outbreak of The Sickness?

He shuddered. The room seemed to cool by a fraction, the difference as sudden as the dissipation of rain. A passing shower, perhaps, isolated in nature? After a quick sip of coffee, he noticed the parsonage darken past the point of the clouded day. "The Sickness," he whispered. Was it already there? Had the sour nausea infected them all?

Darker grew the room, until it evolved hands of its own, until the wind against the shutters whispered to those who might hear. *Colstock...* His name twirled around him, ticking to an unreachable point within his ear, until it became a steady dance, a minuet, as to make mockery of his Holy atmosphere, in what was the most sinful collision he had ever been witness to.

"No!" he cried. "By the grace of the Lord, *No!*"

Ice wind crept upon his back, and spider-like fingers combed through his hair that, of recent, started to thin. The shadow disease caressed and stroked the man, ignoring his cries and pleas to his god and his religion. A thunderous blast sounded from the storm outside, the storm that wasn't, the one he knew had never been, startling Colstock until he nearly tipped the lukewarm cup of coffee into his lap.

Two

A mess of black curls tangled from the humidity hid the noose that hung around the teenage girl's neck and rested against her white lace collar. Purple rosebuds on her patterned dress popped against the clouds that had been lurking in the sky, stalking the spectacle as though they, too, had something to proclaim.

"I didn't do it!" The echo of a dog's bark in the distance was the only sound aside from Bridgette Dawning's insistent protests.

Reverend Colstock used the back of his hand to wipe a bead of sweat from his forehead. *Colstock...* He fished in his pocket until he located a handkerchief. When he pulled it out, the words stared at him. "The Lord is my Shepard, Psalm 23". His late mother had embroidered it as a reminder years ago when he was a boy.

He quickly cleared his throat, his otherwise stern expression softening, just a bit, as his stare met a pair of deep brown eyes. "Samuel Johnson." The reverend's voice struggled to return to a level of professionalism. "This is a serious matter. Are you quite certain you saw *this* young lady playing in Devil's creek?"

Samuel, less eager about meeting the pastor's gaze, glanced down at his furry companion, Bert, who looked up at his master and whimpered. Sam nodded. "Aye, I am."

The reverend lifted his hand. "For Romans, verse six, chapter twenty-three, tells us 'the wages of sin is death.' Redemption lies—"

A loud gasp overcame the crowd as they parted and a craggly figure moved toward the stage. "Lies," she hissed as she approached the platform.

No one in Paradise Grove had heard from Bernadette Withermoore for months. Whispers led many in the town to believe she'd been quietly banished across the creek. Others claimed she passed away, yet no one dared venture as deep into the layers of hawthorn and holly bushes that guarded the woman's house to verify the truth. On that day, however, the gamut of rumors was put to rest as the elderly woman made her way through the onlookers until she stood in front of the wooden platform. Her bony finger shook as she raised it to the girl.

"What lies, dear Reverend Colstock?"

Colstock...come to confession.

No, no. The thoughts grew so loud they escaped the man's pursed lips. "N-no." The crowd gasped, and realizing what he'd done, Colstock straightened his back. He had to regain control of his people.

Lies. The word rang and scraped its way through his ear, and he gently massaged his helix.

"The Lord has spoken; death is the acceptable sacrifice for her sin."

"The Lord?" The woman looked up to the sky and spread her mouth until the width could've easily overcome that of her face. When Colstock looked upon her, he nearly gagged at the yellow hue of crust that stood out against what should've been white teeth. "The Lord!" she cackled.

"Dare you mock messages from the Divine, lady?" He wiped another bout of sweat before continuing. "Dare you mock the vessel through which God communicates?" Another quick massage to relieve the lingering itch deep in the well of his ear. "Shall you join this young girl?"

"Are those *your* lies?"

Colstock, whose cheeks had turned a noticeable red, replied in anger, "Lady, repent that God may pardon your words."

Thunder sounded throughout the dark sky as her wavering tongue stroked her cracked lips. Her hazy eyes cleared, challenging the reverend's confidence to an unspoken duel. *"The Sickness...it's a lie."* Were the last words to escape Bernadette Withermoore's mortal mouth. Leaves rustled, and the thunderous roars created an ominous symphony as the woman's stiff body collapsed to the ground. Gasps and frightened cries were devoured by the crunch of dry grass beneath scattering feet.

The girl's voice shot through the chaos. "I wasn't there...This is all because I—" Frantic sobs mixed with her deep-filled pleas.

Reverend Colstock turned to her. "Silence!" He addressed the crowd. "The Sickness..." As citizens turned to acknowledge him, he continued, "Let this be a warning to all citizens, new..." He nodded to the shell of a body, laying in isolation on the firm ground. "And old." He raised his finger and pointed across the woods. "The Sickness is *there*." He then directed his finger toward the crowd. "And it can be *here*, too, lest we be in fervent prayer and penance to God."

The crowd, ignoring the body of the elderly woman, nodded in agreement. "I saw *him*. I saw *him*. I saw—" the girl turned her eyes to Colstock.

"Take no heed. This is The Sickness, what it does; she is no longer human. She played in the creek of Satan himself. Her eyes, her voice...deception! Generations before us came out of that sinful body of water. My ancestors showed mercy when the Lord asks for the payment of death for our sins."

"Him. Him. Him," she strained, her voice weary from screaming.

Colstock continued over her hoarse cries. "Let today serve as a depressing reminder—that creek is a playground of evil. Second Corinthians chapter eleven tells us, '...for even Satan disguises himself as an angel of light'." The man sighed as the girl behind him writhed and fought to free herself from the binding ropes. Before excusing himself, he turned to the executioner. "Make a quick job of this. There's too much excitement already," he whispered.

A young girl stood behind the safety of a thick oak, far back from the crowd, and watched as the accused dropped abruptly and then kicked and grimaced. After some time, the offender's face faded from deep red to crimson to purplish-blue. Even the struggling slowed, and in its place swayed a limp body. She snorted. Everyone in Paradise Grove grew up knowing the story of Devil's Creek, The Sickness, and how bathing in that creek was like taking a bath with Satan.

Bridgette Dawning looked onward toward the scene. She shook her head and straightened her dress as a few more officers worked with the coroner to untie the pallid body. By the time they lay her straight, much of the crowd had dispersed, partly due to the threat of lightning closing in from the distance.

Bridgette narrowed her eyes and focused on the thicket of trees that acted as a barrier between the city and the creek. Leaves cracked and screeched beneath the soles of her black shoes as she hummed to herself and disappeared into the forest. If anyone had been watching, all they might've seen would've been her dark curls dancing with the cadence of the evening storm.

Three

"Girl!" Mackenzie looked over her shoulder to make sure the overweight woman relaxing in the fluorescent orange lawn chair was, in fact, calling for her. "Yeah! You, girl!" The woman pushed the foot of her cigarette between two ceramic breasts that garnished a risqué ash tray she'd won at last weekend's Texas Hold 'Em tournament and adjusted her lime green visor. The legs of the chair screeched against gravel as she propelled herself from the seat. "Howell's girl, ain't ya?" she called over before waddling closer to the teenager.

"I dunno. What'd he do this time?" Mackenzie folded her arms and waited for the answer.

"Ahh, he ain't done nothing. I was wondering if you were his girl. So many tykes running up and down the roadways nowadays, can't tell. But I'll tell ya what. You walk down the end of the road and grab the mail for me, I'll give ya this." She reached deep into her bra and pulled out a wad of bills.

The young girl pushed some bangs from her eyes and stared at the money. She couldn't count how much was there, but it'd be about enough to grab a hot dog at Corner Store and Market. Her dry lips cracked as a smile spread across her face. "I'd say you got yourself a deal."

The woman nodded and turned back to her lawn chair to lounge until they started pulling Bingo numbers at the club. She grunted as she sorted through the crinkled cash and straightened the bills. In the end it was too much. Back when she was a kid, she wouldn't have asked for one cent to do a kind old lady a favor. She sighed and shook her head before relighting her cigarette and pulling it from the center of the breasts.

"Mackenzie, hey!" Heath ran faster to catch up to her quick pace. "Wait up."

She slowed down and raised her eyebrows at the frazzle-haired boy. "Seriously, *Mackenzie*? He shrugged. "It's Mac, or just don't speak to me. How would you like it if I called you Heathcliff?"

"Ugh."

"So I call you Heath, and you call me Mac. That's our deal."

"Where you going? Your dad's barbequing. Just fired up the grill."

Mac snickered. "Miss Spencer just offered me a wad of cash to get the mail for her."

Heath laughed along with his friend. "'Cause she's too fat to get it herself."

Mac couldn't help but giggle before finally responding. "That's not funny. She could hear you or something."

"Or something," he scoffed. The two of them kicked loose pieces of gravel as they continued down the lengthy driveway to a long row of mailboxes. They finally reached the bottom of the hill and located the one for trailer D13. Heath gave the lid a quick jerk. "Shit," he gasped after a pile of letters flew at him and landed in various places along the rocks. "Does she *ever* get her mail?"

They bent to collect the scattered envelopes. "I don't think she does *anything* unless it involves betting."

Heath nodded in agreement, and they made sure to pick up all the letters. "What you got there?"

Mac looked up. "A hanging."

At first, Heath didn't understand. Mac turned the paper around so he could see the article. "That happened months ago. Paradise Grove, eh? Guess they're crackin' down, huh?"

"Look at her, though. She's our age, and..." Mac's voice trailed.

"And?"

She didn't finish. She centered her attention on Bridgette Dawning's photo. She was a student of beauty and Bridgette, the grand master, the end all be all, a goddess, her goddess. Even within the confines of the black and white square, unlike the photo itself, Bridgette's beauty didn't seem to fade.

"Give it." Heath reached for the paper.

"No." Mac retracted her arm.

"Why not? It's not yours. Why you wanna read about some dead girl."

Without answering, Mac pulled the page from the rest of the paper and tucked it under her shirt. She glanced at Heath and shrugged. "Pages go missing all the time."

Before they headed up the hill, the wind picked up and blew clouds of dirt in their faces causing them to pause and wipe small granules from their eyes. "Ever wonder what it's like to have grass?"

"We have grass. A little, anyways."

"No, I mean like soft, dark green blades of grass. How would it feel to run your bare feet through a meadow? To not be choking from all the dirt and sand all the time. What do you think it's like, Mac?"

Mac hadn't thought of it. Paradise Grove had the grass and emerald hills. Her and Heath would never be allowed over there; they were, after all, descendants of sin, just biding their time on Earth until the Underworld claimed them.

Some days, she'd watch Heath pull a cigarette from behind his ear and light it. Of course, she'd protest that it wasn't healthy. His response was always the same—why should he care? He's going to Hell anyhow; at least he'd get a choice in the way he died.

"Daddy says that if you stand by Devil's Creek, you get glimpses of Paradise Grove between trees in the forest. Especially early in the morning. The rising sun catches on the dew and sometimes it looks like diamonds."

They both stopped and faced one another. "Are you thinking what I'm thinking?"

"If we do this." Mac paused. "We'll risk getting spotted by hunters from across the water. If they see us, they could lie and say we were in the creek. Paradise Grove already hung this Bridgette girl. They ain't playing around anymore. We could die."

"What a way to go, though..."

"Fine, I'm in."

"Mac, you are the coolest girl I know! Tomorrow morning, meet me down there while it's still dark." Before running off to his trailer, Mac could make out a light blush on Heath's cheeks when he took a moment to turn back and wave. "See ya tomorrow," he called out.

Mac was glad to have Heath as a best friend but often wondered how it'd all end. She shivered at the thought. She'd never been like the other girls, sitting in a circle learning to cross-stitch and knit, to cook, clean, to please the man who'd ride up and save her. Didn't anyone understand? There was no salvation. Why get married? To have kids. Why have more kids? They'd have more kids, and more. She, herself, was a third-generation citizen of the trailer-laden satanic step-children of the do-gooders of Paradise Grove.

"Yeah, bring a kid into this damn mess," she muttered under her breath. "Real smart." Even so, most residents thought it an intelligent move—a strategy to get them back into Paradise Grove—that after generations of penance, the lush town across the creek of sins would graciously declare all of them residents, clean from demonic possession, but with each generation came a new group of sinners, some stillborn, others with lung complications, making the satanic curse theory nearly believable.

"You're back, girl." The old lady pulled her sunglasses down and eyeballed the stack of letters. "That's it?"

"All I saw, Ma'am." Mac secretly hoped she hadn't forgotten a few pieces in the dirt but dismissed the thought.

"Okay, set 'em by the ash tray then."

Mac walked up a makeshift sidewalk and as she did, a gust of wind blew a plastic flamingo into her leg. She jumped back.

Miss Spencer gestured with her cigarette. "You ain't gonna make me put this down to straighten it, are ya?"

Mac shook her head and picked up the pink monstrosity and stuck it back into a pile of sand. When she reached the porch, she lay the stack as best she could and waited as the flamboyant woman wrestled her thick hand into her pocket and pulled out the wad of bills.

"Thanks!" Mac responded.

"Yeah, yeah...You best be movin' on home before it gets much darker."

"Of course." Mac folded up the money and headed back to her row. She needed to get to the trailer and excuse herself to bed if she was going to be awake in time to meet Heath by the creek.

She stopped short when she saw her dad shaking hands with Heath's father as burgers sizzled on the makeshift grill. Maybe he bought more scrap parts; that's how her dad earned a living. He left early each day to collect discarded junk from around the area, repair it, and put it up for sale. She shoved the bills deeper into her pocket to avoid questions. Mac hated talking to her dad, and even though he wasn't a bad guy, the sadness she felt for the loss of her mother only fostered a deep resentment for him living and her dying.

"Oh, hey there, Mac. Burger?"

"Nope. Not hungry. Going to bed."

The door slammed behind her, and Howell wondered when and how to break the news to her. He removed the last patty from the grill, placed it on the plate, and sighed.

Four

The woman's voice mixed with fog that surrounded the both of them. Mac studied the ground beneath her, but it was all smoke. The only other figure aside from herself was an elderly lady. "Excuse me?" *Mac took a step closer to the woman whose whisper was inaudible.* "I can't hear you. Speak up?" *She took a few more steps toward the apparition.* "Do you know where we are?"

"The Sickness."

That time Mac could make out what she was saying. "I—I don't know what I can help you with. I'm sorry?"

The woman's face withered. "Lies." *Her scream mixed with the sharp wind.*

Mac all but leaped from her bed. She calmed her breathing. "A dream." Relaxing more, she stood. "A dream," she repeated. She fished underneath her pillow for the stolen newspaper page. After pulling it out, she folded it so only the picture of Bridgette was showing. "Those eyes, though." Had she less sense, she'd have pinned it on her wall, like the posters of celebrities so many girls her age collected from Towne Greene. She sighed. It was a secret, her secret, their secret—Mac and the girl she'd never meet. She blushed. "Too weird," she muttered, all the while staring into the piercing black and white eyes of the photograph for a bit longer before placing it safely beneath her pillow. She resettled herself in bed and drifted into a peaceful sleep.

Several more hours had passed when she woke and sat up, contemplating the trip to the creek. Her dad wouldn't check on her in the morning. That was the one thing Mac was certain of. She thought of the dangers of visiting the banks of Devil's Creek, the recent hanging and once again reached for the article she'd taken from the paper. No doubt about it, Bridgette was a gorgeous dream. "And now you are nothing more than a dream." She stroked the rough paper with her index finger. "Stay safe." She lifted a pillow and placed the article underneath.

Mac sighed. If Heath chickened out on her, it wouldn't be the first time. His habits of concocting daring schemes and failing to follow through with them were tiring. The least he could do would be letting her know, somehow. She took another deep breath and pulled on some jeans and a loose-fitting t-shirt and finished tying her worn-out sneakers before sliding the bedroom window open. She climbed out and dropped down to the rocks.

Mornings were the best time to travel, when the wind was calm. The dust rested along the trail, allowing Mac to take in a clear view of her surroundings. Trailers lined the path until she reached a row of thick but dead shrubbery which extended for as long as she could see. With no sign of Heath in either direction, she searched for something like a clearing, a point where she could avoid getting poked and prodded by the intrusive branches.

After fighting her way through the briars, Mac finally reached a clearing and in brevity, considered calling for Heath. *No, if they hear me, they'll surely come searching.* She looked right and then to the left. Even as the sun made its appearance in the early morning sky, there was no sign of him. Her irritation didn't last too long, though. As the sky continued to brighten, the water caught her attention. It was as beautiful as the rumors made it out to be—clear enough to see the pebbles on the bottom and the sort of deep blue she only explored on the backs of ripped up magazines for sale at Corner Store, destinations nobody in town could afford to travel to except in their imaginations.

Without even putting it to her lips, Mac could tell the water was a cool, sweet song summoning her. She bent closer. *It'd taste like sugar.* Closer. *Sugar with buttered cinnamon*, a bell-like trinkling called her to come closer, to indulge herself in an eerie promise that all she'd ever wanted would come to pass. Just one taste and her desires—the deep longings of her heart, her truth would be granted. *Closer.*

"No." She shook herself from the demonic trance.

She took an abrupt stance, daring the hellishly stunning waters to tempt her once more and, upon doing so, found herself staring directly into a set of eyes bluer than the enticing creek. They were intense against the rich, black hair that hung down the girl's shoulders. Mac hadn't had the fortune of witnessing penetrating beauty in her life but knew even if she had, everything else would've paled in comparison to the vision on the opposite bank. While Mac stood in frozen silence, the girl waved and half-smiled, but then her eyes widened, and she turned and ran into the forest.

"What have I done?" she whispered to herself. Mac started, almost losing her balance and falling in the cursed water. "No, wait—"

"Mac? Who you talking to?" Heath pulled a few stems of California fescue on his way to stand beside her. "Woah, dang...it's just like I heard." Mac looked at him and lowered her brows. "The water, I always heard about the appeal."

"Yeah," Mac half-responded, still thinking about the doll-like girl who had stood before her, the girl from the newspaper. The girl who should've been dead.

"Some say, when it wants someone, it has a way of not letting go—"

Mac huffed in response. "It's water." She leaned her weight toward the creek as though it was pulling her in by the arm. "*Oh, the water got me,*" she mocked. "*Help! I'm withering.*"

Heath shrugged. "It's whatever. That's just what I heard. What were you looking at?"

The girl's deep, thick curls played a loop in Mac's mind. "Nothing." Those blood lips.

"Hmm, not the way you were staring across there. You'd think one of them actors in the magazines was standing over there...or, the Devil himself."

"You're late."

"Oh." Heath put his hands in his pockets. "Change the subject, why don't ya? I stayed up last night. Heard some news, but I'm not gonna be the one to say anything."

"I'm a sucker for gossip."

"No, I'm not the best person to say it."

"C'mon..." Mac's playful tone evolved into an annoyed one.

"No, seriously. Drop it. Sorry I said anything."

She pulled the wad of cash from her pocket. "I'll buy you something at Corner Store." She waved the crumpled bills in front of his face.

He sighed and pushed them back at her. "*No, seriously...*I can't say anything."

"Fine. It probably wasn't interesting." Mac turned and walked through the tall fescue and fought her way through the barrier of shrubs.

Heath struggled to catch up. "Wait, Mac, where you going?"

"To Corner Store, duh," she responded, breaking through the last line onto the dirt road.

"I'm coming too, then," he replied and joined her.

"I don't care. Still not buying you anything, and I'm *not* letting this go."

"I'll buy what I want for myself."

Mac stopped for a second and looked at her friend. "How? You saying you have money?"

"I worked for my dad a few days last week. So, yeah, I have some cash."

"Oh—"

"Hey, guys! Wait up." Georgia's hair flew around with the wind and landed tangled on her shoulders as she finally caught up to her friends. Mac and Heath cleared their throats simultaneously. "Well, what's up? Whatchya doing today? And *what* is all over you two?"

No one really knew how Georgia got her name, but the word, along with her year-round tan skin offset with summer blonde hair and highlighted by light-green eyes, always made them think of warm weather. Needless to say, the name seemed to suit her. Rumors around town suggested that either one or both of her ancestors never ventured into the creek, and her family had only married others who also hadn't touched the water. So, if anyone was to return to Paradise Grove, it'd be her.

Heath spoke first. "Just stuff from the bushes. He shrugged as an attempt to blow the question off. "And down to Corner Store and Market. If you want, I could buy you something. I mean, you don't have to go with us, just…if you wanted to—"

"Don't listen to him. Probably don't have money, anyways. If you want something, I could get it for you," Mac interrupted, smoothing her short, brunette hair behind her ears.

Georgia shifted her weight and didn't answer as the trio continued down the sandy hill and the six blocks through a maze of trailers until they reached Corner Store and Market.

"I dunno why we ever come here." Georgia thumbed through a *National Geographic* that featured macaws. She grimaced at the ripped-up back cover and placed it on the rack in front of a *Motor Trend* magazine. "It's just discarded crap from Paradise Grove." The clerk cleared his throat.

"Mac's idea," Heath chimed in.

"Hey, I earned some cash. Anyway, pick out what you want," Mac offered to Georgia, completely ignoring Heath.

"You know, if we saved it, we could probably afford a trip to Towne Greene." Heath folded his arms over his chest and Mac rolled her eyes.

Georgia stepped in front of them. "Someday, I'll have enough to travel to Towne Greene. I'll pack all my things in a nylon bag, and no one will see me again. I'll sway my luscious hips across an ornate stage, sashaying to my jealous lover's bed. Under the sheets, I'll moan and shake in pleasure while the audience stares, wide-eyed. Juicy nectar drips down my body, and I will autograph my name in His book of success with confectioned beads of sweat, seal it in the fire and blood of stage lighting, and bow ever so graciously to layers of roses and chocolate." She turned back to the others and lifted her eyebrows. "Well...that's more than I can say for *this* town." Georgia dusted off her hands and reached for a pack of gum. "I'll take this."

After a period of stunned silence, Heath spoke up. "I'm gonna get a soda."

Mac ended up buying the gum and the drink but found herself too lost in thought to look for anything herself. Georgia was right in most respects; the way she moved was hypnotic. Without a doubt, she'd be cast in a stage play. Mac, on the other hand, was the polar opposite. At five-foot-six inches, and about one-hundred-twenty pounds, she wasn't tall enough to be considered elegant nor was she short enough to be considered "petite and cute". Her eyes weren't clear and shiny but a dark, murky brown. Freckles danced across her nose, and her brown hair hung a few inches from her shoulders. Nothing exciting there, unlike Georgia's constant mess of blonde curls blowing in an endless rearrangement with the wind.

Mac couldn't decide how she felt about her friend. When the girls first met, she concluded that she harbored a deep hatred for Georgia but figured something more was there because she couldn't seem to keep herself away from her. The past year, Mac felt a semblance of tingles best paralleled to, what she supposed would've been, electric-shock therapy. Being near Georgia was its own form of punishment…in the most wonderful way. It was like someone hanging an unexpired, unopened bar of chocolate near Mac and locking her hands behind her back. Maybe she'd never actually get it and even if she never did, it'd he a hell of a good time just having it dangle nearby, she told herself.

After paying, the three of them stepped out of Corner Store. Heath coughed. "Damn dust."

"Get used to it. Daddy got word of the weather for the next weeks—fifteen mile an hour winds," Georgia offered.

Heath motioned to the cold drink in his hands. "Guess I'll go home and open this inside." He turned the can. "Geez!" The girls leaned toward him in concern. "No. Nothing. It's just that this can is only expired by a month. *One.*"

Mac started walking. "That's lucky."

"Well, this is the closest turn to my place. See you guys."

"Bye, Georgia."

"Yeah, bye."

Georgia's hips swayed as she took a series of sassy steps toward her home, leaving just Mac and Heath. "Now maybe you'll tell me— what *were* you staring at down by the creek this morning?"

"I was looking for the grass. Hoping it'd sparkle." Mac tried to keep her voice even. "Now, I'll ask again. Why were you late?"

"I was up late."

"Doing what?"

Heath inhaled. "Nothing. It was nothing. Talking to my dad. That's all."

Mac raised an accusatory eyebrow. "You stayed up late, and all you did was talk to your dad. I don't believe that."

"It's true."

"No."

"Okay, then you weren't looking at grass."

"Fine, I thought I saw a girl. She was, umm, pretty. It was weird to see a Paradise Grove girl down there."

Heath took a couple steps back. "Stay away from that creek. It's no good. I could feel the evil. It's like all this dust..." He wiped away another swirl of dirt just as the wind picked up. "It just seems to get all over you and when it does, it sticks."

Mac half-laughed. "That's a bit paranoid. I'm going. You're no fun anyway; you've been testy all day."

"Yeah, well—" Heath didn't finish. He couldn't. Didn't want to. "I'm going home. Thanks for the soda." He motioned toward the line of scraggly bushes. "Stay away from that creek." He flashed a warning look and started in the direction of his trailer.

When he was out of sight, Mac shook her head. "Stay away from the creek," she huffed to herself.

The door whined as it shut behind her. "No grillin' tonight. That's a sure bet!" Mac's dad rumbled from the narrow kitchen. "Be sure to kick some of the dust back outside."

"If I open the door again, more will blow in."

The wind howled against the fragile trailer and Howell stepped into the living room, drying his hands on an old rag. "Guess I won't be goin' to work tomorrow. It'll be a good time for us to talk."

Talk? Her dad wanted to *talk*? Mac wondered what this "talking" would entail. She thought about what Heath had told her. How he stayed awake 'talking' to his dad. Her stomach dropped. "About what?"

"You're growing up, Mac." The first thing Mac noticed was how Howell avoided eye contact by looking at his can of beer. "I suppose it's a good time to discuss your future."

Mac's stomach unraveled, and her head throbbed. She knew what the discussion would be. After all, she was seventeen, out of school. The already narrow walls seemed to tighten. Wasn't that what happened to all the girls her age? Of course, it wasn't *what happened* in everyone else's minds, only in Mac's.

"I'm going to bed."

"Not hungry?"

"No." Mac retreated behind the comforter that separated her tiny bedroom from the rest of the trailer. She kicked a few dirty pieces of clothing out of the way and flung herself on the bed. The wind screeched against the otherwise silent, dark room. Her eyes closed, and memories of the intriguing girl streamed through her mind. She pulled the paper from under her pillow and stared at the somber face. "How?" she asked it. "Will I see you again?" She had to know.

She lay on her bed. Yes, she had to know. Those eyes...how could she *not* know? How could she not risk death itself to find out? Georgia's passionate expression of her desire in Corner Store entered her awareness, the sensual intrigue of 'what if' while faced with a life path already drawn out for her.

The "talk" echoed through her head. What of it, though? What if it was exactly what she thought it would be? Is that the end? She'd have no choice. "Yeah, Georgia..." she whispered again, to herself, "I will autograph my name in His book of success with confectioned beads of sweat, seal it in the fire and blood..." Her voice trailed, and she caught herself tracing Bridgette's lips with her index finger.

Mac stood and flicked her lamp on. Howell would usually be awake at eight-thirty in the evening, but he'd drink enough to pass out since he wouldn't be working the next day. Needless to say, he wouldn't be checking up on his daughter. She grabbed a handkerchief and secured it around her mouth and nose. It was a stupid idea, going out in the sand and wind, but it was like she didn't even have a choice.

What was it about girls—about Georgia, about Bridgette—that fascinated her enough to venture out to a demon-possessed creek during the middle of a wind storm?

Sand blew in as soon as she opened the window and hopped out. She gave it a quiet push to close it. The dirt immediately infiltrated the cracks of her makeshift mask, sending Mac into a severe coughing fit. She almost turned around, but the wind seemed to forgive her bad judgement as it slowed. She continued through the darkness, appreciating the lighter wind, and eventually came upon the layers of unforgiving bushes that surrounded Devil's Creek.

With careful footing, she arrived next to the water and looked around—no girl. The clouds separated, and the half-moon cast a light up and down the bank. Still, no one. Why would there be? Maybe she'd hallucinated, or if there was a girl, why would she return? Mac wondered why even she came back.

She turned to leave, but a plink from the water caught her attention. The girl stood on the other side; the moonlight added to the luminosity of her hair. "H-hey," Mac started.

Bridgette didn't respond but just placed her index finger to her lips and turned to an old oak before snapping a long, thick twig. She motioned for Mac to do the same. Though she didn't know why, she too, managed to find a long branch.

Mac broke the silence. "W-what—"

The girl's thick locks of hair shook along with her head. She motioned for Mac to hush and the girl knelt by the water, placing the far tip of the branch inside, and began spinning it in circles. Mac laughed. As long as *she* didn't touch the water, she would be safe.

Mac and Bridgette whirled their sticks around, slow at first, making ripples in the clear creek. They both snickered, quiet at first, but after a while, the giggling turned into nervous, yet satisfied laughter. Bridgette's pace sped up and Mac increased her speed to match; faster, until, after a while, their circles met and eventually the girl's merged with Mac's.

When it did, an intense butterflied-tingle invaded Mac's stomach—the floral ecstasy, nothing Mac had ever experienced. Sweat saturated her forehead; the stick dropped from her hand as it trembled in sync with her legs. Muscles spasmed through Mac's body and lit her insides in a sweet explosion. All the while, the girl maintained a peaceful, satisfied expression.

"Don't stop," Mac cried out right before the fantasy faded to darkness.

On the other side of the creek, the elderly lady from before pointed a finger to the water and then to her lips. She made a "shh" sound. Mac took a step back.

"W-what is it?"

The lady shrieked. "The Sickness...lies!"

Five

Distant mumbling filled Mac's ears. She awoke in a puddle of dry sand in her bed. Did she really go to the creek? Was everything a dream? Why all the sand if it didn't happen? Who brought her back? She reached under her pillow until her fingers met the thin newspaper page. She released a tense breath. When she stood, more dirt fell from her t-shirt and jeans. Exhaustion sank into her mind. Fatigue and weakness almost pushed her to lie down once again.

The feeling, oh. She thought of Bridgette whirling that stick in the cool water, that sugary, refreshing water and that electric vibration that shot through her whole body. She longed to feel that once again.

Mumbles interrupted her fantasy. The quiet voices piqued her curiosity, so instead of returning to her daydream, she pulled the oversized blanket away from the doorframe and exited to the living room.

Howell stood in the corner, arms folded. Heath was asleep on a lawn chair, and Mr. Marshall sat on the couch. Mac's eyes widened. What was going on? Howell was the first to speak.

"You're awake. How're ya feeling?"

"Tired."

His cheeks reddened, and his voice boomed. "What the *hell* were you thinking?"

"W-what do you mean?" Maybe there was still time to save face.

"You know damn well what I'm talking about. You might still be young, but I know you ain't *that* stupid...it wasn't for Heath, you'd probably just be dead out there by the creek."

Heath woke up and Mac took the opportunity to exchange glances with him. He shrugged and said nothing.

Time passed, and Howell moved closer to Marshall. "Don't know what I'm to do with ya." His sigh was defeat incarnate, a summation of everything he'd been feeling since the death of his wife—loss, confusion, especially over what to do with a twelve-year-old girl. Somehow, he'd managed to raise Mac to be a straight-laced young lady, but it seemed, to Howell, even that wasn't going to last much longer. "We've been talking, me and Marshall. You kids are seventeen now, and we think it's about time ya'll get married."

Mac's eyes darted from her dad to Heath. "This...*this* is what you wouldn't tell me yesterday."

Heath stood and started for her. "No. Mac, I just didn't want to—"

Despite the dust storm and her exhaustion, Mac flew from the trailer and fought the harsh gusts, inhaling breaths of sand and coughing up the grains. No, no...they weren't going to make her get married, not to Heath, and for the sake of having a couple stupid babies just to try to better the township.

She quickened her pace. She ran without thinking...without thinking about her circumstance, the threat of marrying a guy who was only a best friend, nothing more, and without realizing where her feet had taken her. She found herself standing at the edge of the cerulean water. Bridgette was there, once again, standing on the bank across from her and indicating that Mac should cross.

"No, I can't. If I get in the water, it'll make me as bad as *they* are." Mac motioned in the direction of her trailer.

The girl pointed upstream to a makeshift bridge. Mac hadn't noticed it before. Bridgette followed her on the other side as she walked toward the conduit. When she arrived, she tapped her foot against the wooden structure. She was confident it hadn't been there during her two earlier visits.

Considering the circumstances, it was of no importance, neither was the fact that Bridgette, the same Bridgette who stood across from her was dead. Things she normally would've questioned, didn't seem to matter. She tapped the toe of her sneaker against it and took one unsure step after another until, despite all legality and past practices, Mac Howell, a girl from the arid trailer park, was officially in Paradise Grove.

The girl, who stood next to her, extended a pale hand. "Bridgette."

Mac accepted it. "Mac." She paused. "But you might already know that." Mac eyeballed the flowered dress. "Is that the only outfit you own or something?"

"I'll live and die in it." Bridgette twirled in a circle and as she did, dark curls caught pieces of sunlight that shattered in Mac's eyes.

Bridgette stopped. "No, do it again." Bridgette giggled and spun once more.

Mac was hypnotized. "Again..."

"No, silly, come take my hand. Come here."

Mac enjoyed taking Bridgette's hand, feeling its cool softness. "Come where?"

"You want to know about grass, don't you?"

Her melodic laugh negated any hesitation Mac would've otherwise conjured. She nodded, and the pair took off through the forest. "If I get caught over here..." Mac glanced down as her shoes sank into patches of deep green grass.

Bridgette joined her and pushed Mac's short hair behind her ear before whispering into it. "A little trust, please?" She batted her bluer than blue eyes.

Goosebumps shuddered up Mac's arms and her stomach went crazy when the warm air filtered through her ear. "I-I can do that."

"Good." Bridgette plopped down and pat the ground, an indication for Mac to also take a seat.

Paradise Grove had no strong winds or sand and dirt to accompany it. Mac took in the rich, green trees. She inhaled a full breath of air and took pleasure in not choking from doing so. In no time, her shoes were off her feet, and she curled and weaved her toes in the refreshing softness. Mac looked toward the countryside. The hill Bridgette had taken them to seemed far away from the community. Mac relaxed, enjoying the soft blades of grass beneath them, and the girls conversed as if they'd known each other their entire lives.

Bridgette watched Mac run her hand over the top of a grassy patch. "It's not as thick as usual. Drought."

Mac whispered, "I don't get you." Bridgette cocked her head. "Seriously, it's like...well, it's kind of like you can read my mind."

Bridgette pushed a piece of Mac's brittle hair behind her ear, and Mac blushed. "You enjoy when I touch your hand, whisper in your ear."

Mac spent a long time debating the response. She could lie, but with the "m" word looming over her, threating to send her days on a downward spiral to what she considered domestic mediocrity, she felt she had nothing to lose. "Can I tell you something?" Bridgette nodded. "It's different. I've never even heard of anything like it. I believe it could be a sinful part of me, probably my ancestral lineage that swam in the creek..."

Before she could continue, Bridgette interrupted. "Say it," she whispered. "Say it and it's yours."

"I think...no, I know, you're the most beautiful person I've ever seen." Mac wanted to delete those words but rambled a follow-up instead. "I mean, I don't know. Maybe this is all wrong. I wouldn't know. Or maybe, if I said that I care for you, it wouldn't mean anything at all—"

The awkward speech was met with unexpected interruption as Bridgette's chilly lips pushed against Mac's, who pressed right back. That was the moment Mac knew—every time she felt tingles around Georgia, each curious action around other girls she encountered, she could only interpret as school girl crushes. The things Mac felt at that moment, with Bridgette grabbing at her hair and Mac's hand running down Bridgette's soft body, meant a significant amount more than anyone she'd ever encountered.

When they parted, Bridgette spoke. "And that meant?"

Mac's lips spread into a smile. "I want to stay." She turned abruptly to Bridgette whose eyes widened in surprise. "Say I don't go back...say I don't. Then what?"

"Anything you desire can happen." Bridgette's eyes seemed to shine until they reached a near-glow.

"But I can't. Where would we go? How...how would we not get caught?" Mac paused for a minute to think. "We'd be together, though, somehow. In the trees, maybe, soaring through wind. We could be birds."

Bridgette laughed. "I hardly have wings, you know."

Mac took a seat next to her and grabbed her hands. "How could you not?"

"Oh, I could easily not. And you, as much as I feel for you, cannot stay." She glanced over her shoulder and could barely make out the parsonage. *Soon, Colstock.* "At least, not yet." She smirked to herself.

Six

The sun had already set, darkening the trail to the creek until Mac found herself hard-pressed to navigate her way across the bridge to the gloom of the other side. She made reluctant attempts to push past the briars and nail-like branches. As soon as she exited the thin forest barrier, she found Heath waiting for her.

"I told you to stay out of there!" he yelled against the howling wind. "You just keep returning. Why, Mac? *Why*? Do you *want* to die?"

Before she could answer, Heath grabbed her arm and started walking until they arrived at a small tin shed. He pulled her in with him to a corner to protect them from the wind. "I like it there. I enjoy the glimpses of Paradise Grove," she lied. "You *told* me to?" He shrugged. "*Told?*"

Heath moved closer to her and placed a hand on her arm. He'd never done that, and she wasn't sure how to interpret the gesture. "I know you don't want to get married. I don't either; I mean, not now. Maybe at some point." He exhaled a deep breath. "But I thought about it, and if I'm forced to marry anyone, I'm glad it's you."

"Heath, we can fight this—"

"And what? Travel to Towne Greene? This town has few rules, marriage being one. You know that." Heath sighed. "I'm sorry. We should just go with it and hope that our kids get a better chance. Maybe, together, we can make it better."

"Kids?" Mac fumed at the notion. "*Kids?*" The thought of having children taunted her mind. "I'm *not* having kids."

"One step at a time. We both know there's no getting out of this." Heath pushed a short piece of bang from Mac's forehead, but that swarm of emotion she'd felt from Bridgette was nonexistent with Heath. "One step at a time. Yes?"

His forehead crinkled as his eyes met Mac's. "I—" She turned away.

Maybe that moment was right. Maybe it was Heath, and everything with Bridgette was wrong. She thought about what Bridgette told her earlier that she could have anything…anything she wanted. She wanted Bridgette. But she couldn't stay in Paradise Grove, and why would Bridgette want to move to trailer park hell for her?

Maybe, Mac was playing on a whim, on a notion that would never come to fruition? Had her entire life not been heartbreak? Wasn't the adage that past behavior was the best predictor of the future? And if so, would it be fair if she gave Bridgette a chance earlier that day and never extended the same opportunity to Heath. After all, they'd been lifelong friends. What would it hurt if she tried to have feelings for him? Mac made up her mind; the next day she'd sneak off and talk to Bridgette.

***

Mac was startled. In the distance stood a figure. Delicate purple flowers speckled the girl's dress. "Bridgette?" *Mac questioned. Without responding, the girl turned and walked away. Where was she? She looked around, but darkness was the only background that met her gaze.* "Wait!" *Mac tried to scream, but words caught in her throat and burned. It was being crushed, and she wasn't sure what was causing the sensation.* "My throat."

The girl stopped and turned. It was Bridgette, but that time her eyes were ablaze with warning. Her urgent voice broke through the thick void. "Stop seeing me, Mac." *Bridgette's cheeks seemed to have a blush they didn't have the day before. Her energy was warmer. Her plea grew in desperation.* "Don't see me."

"Bridgette, why?" *She neared Mac and took both of her hands into her own. Mac asked once more.* "Why?"

Bridgette's blue eyes widened. "*Because, she's not me,*" *she whispered.* "*Stay away from her, from that thing, from all of it. It won't bring me back to you.*"

Mac was still grasping at her throat as she jerked up in bed. Sweat beaded across her forehead. Sun and dirt streamed through the thin curtain. Morning. She wiped some pieces of hair from her face.

"If Bridgette wasn't Bridgette...then..." After an incredulous blink she returned to the question at hand.. "Then, who is Bridgette?" The thought caused her head to start pounding, the thought or the dirt or both.

Seven

Elijah Colstock leaned against the east wall of the sterile cottage. "You are saying there is no remedy?"

Theophilus, Paradise Grove's apothecary, studied him before answering. "Tell me, there is no history in all your family of this ringing in the ear?"

"No. Of course not. No Colstock has ever suffered such ailments as this. Were that the case, who would make a proper job of sharing the Lord's word?"

The druggist took a seat behind his cluttered desk and glanced at the pale man over his glasses. "Uh huh," he mumbled. "Had I to guess, I would venture toward there being a familial link with this affliction. This ringing you speak of, it would typically be passed down generationally. Perhaps it is a fleeting nuisance?"

Colstock made his way to the door. "Yes, you may be correct in your thoughts. For that, I show appreciation. I do ask, however, speak of this to no one. I will take my leave."

Colstock had spent countless nights awake, contemplating his inevitable visit to seek out medical treatment. If questioned by someone in Paradise Grove, how would he respond? What cover would he seek? Implying that anyone who inquired could've been contaminated with The Sickness might just have been the antidote to curiosity.

As he started down the sidewalk, his body nearly buckled beneath a great weight. The burden wasn't physical in nature, but more so it existed in unseen bricks on some invisible plane. The heaviness had seemed to increase in the weeks prior.

He glanced up to the threatening clouds that masked the afternoon sun. "Why won't it just rain," he muttered to himself while surveying the fields of once lush, green grass. Of late, they had thinned and faded to a yellow-green. Where once a person could stroll above a soft carpet, the blades crunched as though they were shards of glass fighting to remain in one piece.

His attention turned to his ear. The tickling mosquito buzz that nestled in an unreachable pocket refused to diminish.

Colstock...

The pastor scratched his forehead and took another step.

Colstock...

His ear hummed. For a moment he believed the appendage to be an insect, ready to detach and fly off into the humid air. *Keep walking,* he thought to himself. His body grew heavier than before.

You would ignore me?

The sharp ring clawed from the inside out and he rubbed the side of his ear using his knuckle before shifting to his fingertip. He allowed his short but sharp nail to take brutal digs into the thick skin that served as a barrier between the outer world and the source of the nuisance. Someone had planted a seed. It took root. It sprouted, and the stem grew tall and widened each day.

Fool you are to ignore me.

His feelings were rooted in something of a nightmare. *Perhaps The Sickness has made a legitimate return. Ringing of the ear could be the first symptom.* His thoughts became reality he spoke aloud. "I should confide this in someone. But who?"

The seconds ran a race with his mind. Colstock's return to the village was all too sudden. The time had not passed noon and open-air stands offering a gamut of products from soaps to fruits and vegetables littered each side of the road. To the citizens of Paradise Grove the scene was a modest illustration of an ordinary day. To Colstock, it was a red carpet. Repositioning his shoulders, head held high with the pride of several generations of Colstocks to back him, he commenced his arrogant stroll down the dirt path.

As he expected, merchants and shoppers alike came to a halt as the man of God made his way among them. He smiled and nodded, occasionally saying a near-genuine "hello" or "God bless". From head to toe, he bathed in celebrity and made a mental note to frequent town at more regular intervals.

A few of the women competed for eye contact. In many ways their attentiveness served him well. With his chest out, he managed a coy smirk and to shower each one by looking them straight into their eyes as though he was already promising courtship. Of course, he wasn't. They didn't know that. They never would.

You enjoy the attention, do you not?

Ignore it, he thought to himself.

"Pastor..." The words faded into his awareness.

He worked to rub out the nail-like scratching from his ear, and his eyes met a woman's deep brown ones. He forced a smile. "Yes."

He hadn't noticed the contents in her hands until she outstretched a wrapped loaf of bread. "It's fresh." Her cheeks filled with color. "I made it and would like you to have it."

"Oh, I..." His voice trailed as his stare tore from her eyes and focused on his peripheral where Samuel stood outside a local tavern, a wide grin embedded on his face that grew larger at Leonard Torrelson's words. Colstock clenched his jaw, refusing to allow the situation to cause outward vexation. "M-my apologies." Quite out of the usual, his words staggered as he tried to maintain appearances and keep an eye on the delicate situation between the two men in the corner. "I uh..." he took the loaf. "May the Lord continue to bless you."

She giggled. "Why, thank you, Pastor Colstock."

He acknowledged her with a swift but polite nod and hastened to his parsonage, his refuge. Fury seemed to exacerbate the tickling sting that plagued his ear, causing it to ring and buzz until he had little choice but to take a seat.

Eight

Colstock sat in the parsonage, alone; venomous thoughts of Samuel and Leonard plagued his mind. The round clock that had kept faithful time ticked an irritating tempo in sync with the popping in his ear.

*Colstock...*hummed its way into the crackling.

"I will not be infected with your sin."

Oh, but you will, dear, dear pastor. The voice was a hiss that chilled Colstock's ear.

"I will *not!*" The 'not' echoed loud enough to almost drown out an unexpected knock on the wooden door.

He comes...

"Who comes?"

Another knock.

A quick pain shot through Colstock's head when he shook it. "Please, come in," He called, straightening himself.

The door spoke of little except a need for a good oiling of the hinges as it opened. The pastor's eyes widened before his expression softened. Samuel Johnson studied the room. "I wasn't aware that you had...company?"

Colstock stood. "No, and I was not expecting such." He crossed the room until he was standing next to Samuel. "It seems you lack an issue finding companionship."

Ignoring the latter remark for the time, he narrowed his brows and questioned. "Then to whom were you speaking?" Samuel took another glance around the humble perimeter.

Oh, Colstock, why don't you tell him? Why do you lie about our afternoon interludes?

"I do not lie—" Samuel looked on Colstock with a questioning expression. The pastor wiped a bead of sweat from his forehead before it had a chance to linger and continued, "I was speaking about Sunday's sermon. Lies, they're the beginning of The Sickness that hangs a threatening cloud above Paradise Grove."

Colstock's eyes followed Samuel's hand as he reached up and cupped the pastor's cheek in his palm. "Do you not think we have lied? As for your last question, I take you to be referring to my previous conversation with Leonard." Colstock broke his gaze and turned from the man. Samuel repeated with authority. "Do you not believe we have lied?" Time passed. "Answer me." Colstock turned back but did not speak. "Answer me, Holy man. For this is what young Bridgette Dawning lost her life to protect. This secret. The lie. *Our* lie. A lie I no longer care to live."

The man's lips quivered, but his demeanor did not break. "You know not of what you speak."

"I am aware of what I speak. I speak to truth. What is your hesitation of expressing how you think on me? In public, I am meaning."

Yes. A bony finger traced its way up Colstock's neck. *"Colstock...tell us...what is the truth?"*

"The church," was all Colstock could muster.

Samuel shook his head. That answer would not suffice. "While I dare say our predisposition might be unique, it is accepted. They will accept us. What is it *really*? Tell me, are you drowning so deep in your lies you can no longer see the surface? This "Sickness" of yours, of your family's, is it not too a lie?"

The clock's reverent tick followed by an eager tock caused the pastor to, once again, reach to his ear and scratch the skin where the cartilage met his jawline. "Over one hundred years of the Colstock family has led this church, these people. They are my people, *mine*. I refuse to lose all we have built for a few clandestine, fleeting moments in the woods with you, Samuel Johnson."

"So, these lies you tell, they are for the grandeur? They are to keep your celebrity, the clamor that ensues when the Godly reverend Elijah Colstock makes his way through Paradise Grove. For this notoriety, would you lie, murder?" Samuel shook his head. "Of you, I thought better." He scoffed. "Consider me finished." His boots shook the weakened floor as he stomped out of the room.

Your lies spread disease. Innocent blood spilled upon your word, the voice hissed.

"I cannot hear you."

But, you can.

"I cannot." Colstock grabbed at his ear.

You do.

"Upon my word, I do not." He reached to his ear again, and blood trailed behind his unfiled nails. "I will not."

You will.

"Will..." he grunted and scratched once more, "not."

You will hear the lies that you have spread. You will face them.

Another sharp pass at his right ear and Reverend Colstock's body thumped to the floor, heard only by Samuel who, after quick thought, turned back to the parsonage for a final word. Upon whipping the door open, he witnessed the silent body.

"Elijah!" He ran to the reverend. "Elijah?" He checked the neck to find a pulse. "Hear me, now. For you're not dead. Not yet."

He struggled to collect the unconscious reverend and deliver him, in haste, to the infirmary.

Nine

Mac waited until the sun had fully set behind the trailers before sneaking out of the window. A new thought entered her mind; she'd have to return long before morning. Howell would be checking in, and when he didn't find her there, panic would ensue.

As much as she tried to ignore the whispers behind her back, she knew they were, indeed, as true as the reality she was facing. How long, she wondered, would it be before residents started realizing she had ventured across the creek? And how much time did she have until the news reached Paradise Grove? What then?

Twigs from the unforgiving shrubs scratched and tore at her t-shirt as though they, too, were grasping to pull her back to everything that should've made sense but didn't. She ripped the debris away and her hair pulled and crackled as she brushed through it with her fingers.

The moon lit the way down the narrow creek bed. When she reached the other side, Bridgette met her with a hug. They separated, and Mac studied her. Each time they had an encounter, she looked the same, except in the dreams. In the dreams, her snow-white cheeks were touched with a light blush, her skin warm, and her warning urgent. *Just stay away*, she'd insist. But Mac couldn't.

Bridgette's forehead crinkled. "What's wrong?" Mac stepped back. "It's like you've seen a ghost."

Or a demon, the voice broke into Mac's consciousness.

Mac blinked. "What? I don't..."

Bridgette reached a porcelain hand to wipe a few pieces of stray hair from Mac's forehead, but Mac pushed her away. "Are you okay?" Bridgette studied her confused expression.

Mac's mind spun. What was she doing? Who was Bridgette? Was Bridgette truly a 'who', after all?

"Come on, silly. Let's find our spot and relax." Bridgette offered an eager hand, and Mac tried not to display any subtle reluctance to accept.

Bridgette led them to the same soft spread of grass as before. Mac took a look around and noticed what Bridgette had been talking about—the drought seemed to be turning the once green field to lighter shades of yellow.

Once they settled, Mac weaved a long stem of grass in and out of her fingers. "I have to tell you something, and I don't want to."

"Then don't." Bridgette leaned in, and their kiss lingered amid the concert of cicadas and croaks of frogs. Despite the pleasant evening breeze, Bridgette's skin was ice. Mac held her tighter, hoping to warm her.

After a while, she spoke up. "I feel like I should give Heath a chance, you see. Where I'm from, no one lives if they don't marry," Mac finished the apologetic explanation to Bridgette before sneaking another soft kiss.

"This simply cannot be." Bridgette thought for a moment. "What about another city? Towne Greene, is it?"

Mac released a deep breath. "It's far from both towns. At least a day away. That's if you can afford a bus or have the nerve to leave in the first place. Once you do, it's like you alienate yourself—you become an outsider. People know you, but they won't act like it if you return for a visit. You know—"

"But *we* could be together."

Mac never understood the phenomenon of how Bridgette's voice, her words, her body, could lure her as though she were a siren Mac once read about in pages of a torn novel Corner Store lent out until the book's mysterious disappearance. Something about Bridgette tempted her to bend to whatever the girl asked of her, and moreover, made her happy in doing so.

Bridgette lowered her voice to a whisper and pulled Mac's hair back. "We could have *everything*," she whispered in Mac's ear. "Things your friends only dream of—grass, a home, unexpired food, new magazines. What can I offer to you, my love? Come with me, and I'll fulfill your every want. Promise me your life, your soul, and in return I promise you all your desires."

Don't listen to her, a voice broke in.

Mac turned to locate the person it was coming from but only found an empty swath of grass. She squinted to see better but found nothing. She looked away from Bridgette. "Did you hear that?"

Bridgette turned Mac's head, forcing her attention, and continued in her seamless whisper. "Tell me," she hissed. "Promise me." Her eyes nearly glowed. "Swear to it."

Mac's stare was blank for some time. *She's trying to control you.*

Despite the thrilling sequence of goosebumps trailing down her neck and extending to her arms, the idea that she could be bought or somehow bribed infuriated Mac. Her stance was abrupt. "Love." She straightened her shirt and pulled her hair from her face. "That's everything I need. Love is not a barter. You wouldn't be selfish enough to make it harder for me to do what I feel is fair if you loved me. You would wait!"

Don't look at her.

Bridgette also stood and snuck up behind Mac. She placed a cool, soft hand on each of her shoulders. "Mac…" she whispered.

Mac inhaled a deep breath and held it. She could fight; she didn't know why, but she had to resist.

Run, now!

Bridgette rested her head on Mac's shoulder. "Mac..." She pulled her short hair back so she could have better access to Mac's ear. "Who's been talking to you?" came her sweet voice.

"How? What?" Mac stepped back from Bridgette.

She maintained a calm disposition. "What have they told you?"

Run, Mac!

"Who is it?" Her impatience grew. "Who's telling you things?"

"How did you—"

Stop talking to it. Run, now!

Mac refused to look at Bridgette. Instead she turned and fled, fast. Bridgette's pleas hung themselves in the evening air. "Mac!"

She didn't let them impact her. She continued across the bridge, through the forest, past the long field of rocks and dirt, to Heath's trailer. Her relentless pounding caused more than one light to come on in the otherwise dim row of trailers.

She paused her frantic knocking to notice the barks of dogs. There'd be talk the next day. "Let them talk," she whispered and shoved strands of hair from her face.

The door opened mid-knock to Heath as he yawned and pressed his eyelids together to allow his vision time to adjust. "Mac?" he cocked his head in confusion.

"Heath." She threw her weight into him, knocking them both inside the trailer. "Maybe I was wrong about it all. What if they're right?"

He scratched his head. "Huh?"

"They could be right." Her eyes were wide and matched her wild hair.

"You're, uh, you're not making sense."

"About getting married, giving each other a chance. What you said, like we're both not ready to be married, but if it's the law then, I'd rather be married to you."

He stepped back and took a few moments to study the tears and shakiness of his childhood friend. "You sure?"

Mac shook her head. "No."

Heath wrapped his arms around her and whispered. "Me neither."

The two of them stood like that for what could've been hours, both speculating the what-if's, both cursing an archaic law thought to push citizens into a Holy contract recognized by a god that had been said to have abandoned them.

Ten

"I cannot lie, for it is these lies that have ended us all in hopelessness. Lies are death and all the destruction left in its path."

Mac blinked and tried to look deeper into the nothingness. "I don't understand."

"Focus. You will."

A scene appeared in front of her, and Mac found herself peering from around a tree. She studied the familiar area; it was the forest that separated Paradise Grove from Devil's Creek.

"Bridgette, come back! It's not that important!" She turned to see a redheaded girl call down from the beginning of the tree line. "Spooky lady Withermoore lives down there."

"Janet, I'm the one who hit it this far." On the other side of Mac stood Bridgette.

Mac whispered, "Bridgette?"

The girl didn't hear her. "I'll get it."

The redhead tossed her curls behind her back and stuck a hand on her hip. "Fine. But I'm leaving. I will not be a party to this…sticking around for Withermoore the Witch to snatch me up and cook me."

"Then go," Bridgette snapped before turning to continue into the woods. To herself, she commented, "Now, where did it go?" Her eyes searched the forest floor. In the distance bushes rustled. The girl gasped and took a few steps backwards.

"Then, tell me these words, that I know them, that I may cherish them. Tell me, Colstock, speak to me these feelings." Upon hearing the voices, Bridgette sunk behind the same tree where Mac was hiding. Both girls watched two men engaged in what seemed to be an intense conversation.

"I shall not. These words you know." Colstock softened his voice and sighed. "Samuel Johnson, for the words I have for thee, these feelings, they are, at best, forbidden."

"By whom? No, be it not so. For the truth—"

Whatever Colstock was about to say went unknown. A minor shift of weight caused a twig to snap beneath Bridgette's shoe. The men turned at the sound, and the narrow trunk of the tree revealed a head of black curls.

The reverend approached. "And this?"

Samuel Johnson walked behind the girl. "Bridgette Dawning..."

"What did you see?" Colstock snarled.

"Please," Bridgette begged as though she was already aware of her fate. "I will speak of this to no one."

"You will not, child." Colstock neared her and grabbed her arm, leading her up the path and into the meadow.

Though the trio had walked out of her sight, Mac found herself unable to move. The dream wouldn't end. Why? Her heartbeat sped. *There's more here*, she thought.

A burst of wind caught her attention and she looked to her left where an elderly lady wobbled from a group of trees. "Lies," she said, "for only destruction can come through their lies." She looked to the creek as a dark figure emerged from the waters. Mac gasped, and the lady continued in a quivering voice. "For their lies will manifest bleakness, the energies from hell itself. Take me at my word." Her face met Mac's and revealed a clouded eye.

Mac woke with a jump and silenced herself before she screamed and disturbed her dad. "Lies," she whispered. "Is that what happened to Bridgette?" Was that Bridgette? The Bridgette in her dreams? The Bridgette at the creek? "Bridgette's dead." She pulled the old newspaper from under her pillow. "Dead." She hit the photograph with her fist. "You are dead." The paper screamed as she ripped it once, twice. When finished, Mac reached to the floor and gathered up the pieces and tossed them in the trash. "And now I know why you're dead."

She sat on her bed for several moments, just to feel herself breathe. The wind pounded small rocks and dirt against the walls of the trailer, but even that relaxed her. Like breath, the troublesome sound served as another aspect of life she could rely on when all else seemed to be crumbling around her. After some time, she grabbed the torn photograph from the waste basket and searched her desk for a roll of tape.

Eleven

It was a bright Sunday. The message on the board in front of Paradise Grove Church read, "Pray earnestly for rain, lest we prepare our fields upon deaf ears", which, following his ordeal at the infirmary that consisted of several stitches and bandages, Colstock did not find amusing.

Knowing the congregation was already questioning such an incident that had happened earlier in the parsonage, he took his time dressing himself in Holy garments. "Rain," he remarked to himself as he tended to adjusting the collar of his robe so it was straightened to a level of perfection that none dared gossip of. "It must rain soon." He took a tedious moment to inspect himself in the full-length mirror attached to the door. "A storm would serve as an effective distraction."

Mocking laughter interrupted his silent moment, sounding from behind him. Colstock spun to see who it could be. Nothing.

Colstock...

"Be gone with you. This is a place of the Lord," he commanded.

More laughter. *Oh, dear Colstock, was it not you who summoned me?*

"I know not of what you speak. Be gone." He wiped tears of sweat from his forehead. "Know it not, Colstock, for speaking to it gives it your power."

A family with a legacy of lies... A shrill cackle and then, *Lies, lies, lies, lies...*

Elijah Colstock covered his ears in an attempt to protect them from the repetitive words and finished buttoning the cuffs of his sleeves. "I will talk to you no more." He stepped from the door that led to the church sanctuary and wiped a stream of sweat before taking his place behind the wooden pulpit.

The silence of the congregation was cumbersome. On a normal Sunday, he would have embraced it as a sign of respect, but that day, the stillness served as a reflection of curiosity, rumors that seeped through the stained-glass windows and circled amid the calm. What happened to Pastor Colstock's ear? What did he do to it? Their minds were ticking clocks of speculation, that much he knew.

Tick, tick…Colstock…

He shut his eyes for no more than a second and reopened them, but the steady ticking didn't leave his awareness. The noise was somewhere in the pursed lips of the woman in the third row, and it bounced off the balding head of the man sitting in front of her. Didn't they notice?

More sweat dripped from his hairline, down his forehead. He wiped it away and swatted at a buzzing fly that zipped by his right ear before he cleared his throat to begin. The sound ricocheted off the painted widows, the large doors, and straight back to Colstock, causing a sharpness to echo through his mind.

Tick…Tock…

No, he thought. *Not that day. Not on the day of the Lord.* His mind absorbed the subtle rhythm until it would no longer leave him. *The Word*, he needed the Word. As he tucked the handkerchief back into his pocket, the verse caught his eye. He gently rubbed his itching ear and began.

"'The Lord is my shepherd; I shall not want. He maketh me to lie—'" The fly returned to his side, making itself comfortable next to his temple. It buzzed with a level of rage that directly contradicted the serenity of the congregation. The nuisance circled around Colstock's head, and he swatted at it in vain.

Colstock, pray tell, what of your lies? The "s" slithered into the preacher's ear, and he rubbed at the bandage that covered it. *For the clock does tick...*

The reverend cleared his throat. "'—down in green pastures: he leadeth me beside the still waters. He restoreth my s-'"

Colstock... The buzzing crescendoed. Colstock rubbed at his ear with force, but the bandages were becoming a menace. Despite a few murmurs in the congregation, he removed a layer so that he could reach the source of his discomfort.

"Continuing on. 'He restoreth my soul: he leadeth me in the paths of righteousness for his name's sake. Yea, though I walk through the valley of the shadow of—'" His ear buzzed and swarmed. No amount of pressure seemed alleviate the piercing itch. "'Yea, though I walk through the—'"

The needled sensation swarmed his external auditory canal until something in Colstock's ear popped.

The hand reached the hour mark; his time was up. "No, it can't be." His incoherent mumbling wasn't heard by the congregation. The sound of the ringing clock thundered through the tympanic membrane and what was left of the bandages soaked up warm liquid that seeped to his auricle. He rubbed at his ear, unable to satiate the sharp tickle. "'—valley of the shadow'" He continued with haphazard.

He didn't notice the shocked expressions, nor did he hear the whispers that surfaced throughout the congregation as he removed the moist covering, letting it fall to the floor. Dark yellow liquid streamed from his canal and down his neck, only stopping when it reached the collar of his once white shirt. The desperate scratching at his auricle exacerbated the spectacle as blood mixed with the sallow puss. He spoke louder as he continued to gouge at the source of his suffering. "'—shadow of death, I will fear no evil...'"

Can you dig deeper, Colstock?

"I can't hear you," he grunted, pushing deep enough into his ear canal to scrape out blood when he pulled his fingers back. The itch was insatiable; it was something that ticked and infiltrated his being. *Flies*, he thought. It was all the flies inside him that needed to come out. "Pull them out," he said to himself, digging even deeper than before.

No one in Paradise Grove Church that Sunday morning dared move from their seats. Disgusted parents covered their children's eyes. Some were mesmerized by the sight of their pastor progressively losing his mind right before their eyes; others believed God himself came down upon them as a test of faith, that through the near-fantastical display of horror, the Lord was working through Colstock to purge their sins.

Deeper, Colstock...

"Shut up!" The Pastor turned and yelled at the nothingness behind him, "Shut up and set them free!" Colstock, who had exchanged scratching at the flies hidden somewhere deep within him for repeated pounding at the side of his head with his fist, crumpled to the floor.

A few whispered prayers broke through the blood-stained silence, and still everyone looked on. Many believed that through some Divine miracle, Colstock would get up and preach once again. When he didn't, someone yelled, "Get help!"

A hesitant Samuel Johnson approached, and a few more men joined him. Amos Harper moved the pastor's hand to reveal his ear dangling from the lobe. Samuel pushed the Bible away from the scene to protect it from staining.

Twelve

Mac sat in front of her dresser mirror. From the kitchen she heard, "Oh Mac, darling..." as it sang its way through the makeshift door. She'd spent the morning staring at the picture of the dead girl in the newspaper. Was she making the right choice? The drawer clicked after she folded the paper up and shoved it inside. Weeks had passed since she ran from Bridgette. The only comfort came from her dreams.

More than a few times, Howell expressed his concern about her sleeping as much as she had been. She responded by ignoring him. When she slept, she saw Bridgette, danced with her, talked with her. And that Bridgette, the one who came to her each time her eyes closed, was warm and glowing.

"And if that's all I ever get, I guess I'll—"

An inaudible voice came closer. "And she comes, swaying to the lust-ridden alter of forever, a virgin blush glazing her cheeks, her bosom ready to burst with the want of, the need of—"

She turned to acknowledge her friend as she sashayed into the bedroom. "Really, Georgia?"

Georgia's blonde hair bounced as she jumped on the bed. "So...whatcha got? What are you wearing? Hair? Makeup? What?"

Mac shrugged. "Don't know. Don't really care, even. I mean, does it matter, G? Will it make any difference?"

"Well, hell." Georgia released an exasperated sigh. "Go naked."

Mac scoffed.

"Heath is good looking." Georgia sat up on the bed. "He's hot. Everyone thinks so. Probably one of the best-looking guys to snag in the area. What's the problem?"

"What if—" Mac thought for a moment. What if she told Georgia? What if she spilled everything to her friend? About liking women, about Bridgette, about her dreams.

"What if, what?"

"Nothing."

Georgia jumped from the bed and hangers clicked as she fished through Mac's closet. "Here," she presented, spinning around with a black dress.

"It's *black*."

"Good!" She dusted it off. "It fits your mood. Now. Put it on."

Mac took the dress and stared at her friend. "Excuse me."

"Fine! I'll leave. See you outside."

Mac undressed and changed into the dark atrocity. "Damn," she sighed and sat on the bed. "Damn..."

Thirteen

Samuel Johnson stood over Colstock's hospital bed. "W-wh—" Elijah Colstock struggled to sit up.

He offered the pastor a cup of water. "Here, don't drink fast."

Colstock took it and sipped. "You can't be here," he whispered. "Don't you know that?"

Samuel leaned back. "You would reject me?"

Colstock's eyes softened at the realization of Samuel's dejection. "No, I did not mean it for rejection. But these things...the intrigues...well, we need to tread with delicacy."

"And will we not ever be able to indulge, to partake of each other in the day's light?"

"No," he hissed. "We shall never."

Samuel flinched and shifted his weight. "Then..."

Colstock leaned toward him, but Samuel put his hands up and turned before exiting the sterile room.

"Sam—" But Colstock couldn't get the words out fast enough. Samuel was gone. He swallowed; he wouldn't be returning. A shrill stab consumed his body. He hurt; not physically but in every other way he could be hurt.

A nurse rushed into the room. "Now take it easy, you. Let's take a look at you."

"Sam..." It was as those words left Colstock's mouth that he noticed the drumming echo through his head. He turned his attention to the nurse who took care to lift and unwind the dressings. "What of this echo, lady?"

"Reverend, it's an act of the Lord himself that you are still with us." She spoke as she hustled to monitor and record his vital signs. "But your ear...just wasn't part of God's plan. I was in church that day. I knew something awry after you came to the pulpit. You all but went from pale to ghost white, and I knew, I told myself, 'Piety Harmon, there is something wrong with Reverend Colstock'." She huffed and put her hands on her hips. "But did I do anything about it? No. Of course not. Well, it's just a wonder you're alive. If I say nothing else, allow me to say that much."

Piety turned to grab some ointments from her cart to apply to the wound. As she prepared the salve, the startled man felt the side of his head. His fingers explored a flat, sewn up layer of skin where an ear should have protruded.

She moved his hand from the wound. "You don't need to be touching that without gloves lest you infect it, and I say, you infect an open sore such as this, you will have hell to pay...pardon my language. I've seen such things before. Of course, in my line of work, we see all. We experience all there is to experience. I tell myself a lot, 'Piety, you sure have seen your share of infections.' Them bubbling, blistery, puss-fill—well, never you mind. If I say nothing else, though, mind yourself touching that place until it his well healed." When he didn't respond, she continued to tend to his ear and hurried to redress it with more bandages. "Well, lunch is about ready, and I'm sure you're famished. I'll return in short." The nurse shuffled about the room for a while. Colstock only knew when she finally left because the door clicked when she closed it behind her.

*Colstock...*Despite his recent loss, the voice came through with clarity. *Tick, tock, tick...*

The pastor swallowed. "You have done enough damage to my town—" Laughter caused his head to swell. "—to my people."

You have done this to your people...your generations of deception.

Colstock sat up. "Enough!" he managed to raise his voice despite the fatigue.

Wild shrieks filled the hospital room as a chill crept up the man's skin beneath the paper-thin gown. Goosebumps trailed up his legs and arms and a fly buzzed around his neck.

"In the name of God, be done," he called to the shadows that suffocated his space. The man trembled. "Be done with you, evil being."

Light entered as the door opened. "What of this?" The busy nurse studied the man's wild eyes and frantic motions. "Whatever are you swatting at?"

Colstock's frightened lips wavered, and his body shook. "W-wh..."

The nurse placed the tray on a table. "Reverend?" The man's answer was a blank, frantic stare. "Okay, I'm getting the doctor."

Shadows soaked into the room as she took her leave. *Colstock...* The menacing voice taunted the man who remained still, unblinking, unknowing and devoured by generations of Colstock family secrets just as a mountain of flies consumed the lunch since abandoned by the nurse. The patty of meat opened, and more insects climbed out, creating a black mound where food once sat. Some rained down on the floor and crawled about the room.

The fly landed in the space between the pastor's eyes. *Colstock...* it taunted him, ticking its way into his consciousness. The chilling cadence caused him to sweat and shiver.

He tried to swat it away, but the menace wouldn't budge. "No!" he cried out in panic. "Just, no!" His legs grew restless and he kicked at the air and batted at his face. He tried everything he could manage to ward the evil from him. "Father God." Still trembling, he closed his eyes and folded his hands in prayer. "Father God!" he called out, even louder.

Sweat tickled his cheeks as he refused to break his prayerful position to wipe it off. "Save me, *Father God*," he wailed. "Do not forsake me."

The door opened once again, and a doctor hurried in along with Piety. "Doctor." Her eyes were wide and frantic.

"A reaction, to the medication," he diagnosed. "It must be. The man is wild, uncontrollable...quite out of character."

"Do you believe he has." She paused, afraid to say the next few words. "The Sickness?"

The doctor removed his glasses and studied Colstock. "Think not of it. No Sickness shall defeat the faith of Pastor Colstock, for he is earnest in his relationship with God. He is honest. His integrity and righteousness shall be his salvation."

"Then, I'll give him a shot, an antidote to the medication."

"Yes, and with haste lest he causes more damage to himself. For this truly must be a test of God, and we must do our part in faith, good nurse."

Fourteen

Time passed; sometimes there was too much of it and other times, not enough. For Mac, the latter was true of nights, where, as she slept Bridgette met her. In warm fields of soft grass and flowers the girls could simply be—together, lost in slow, deep conversation, holding one another, laughing, carefree. Night was the incentive for Mac to survive the day. But, very much like the evening's darkness, shadows of her clandestine encounters smothered any light that might have come from her daytimes.

Heath started a new job working in the trash yard. Eight-hour days turned to ten hours and twelve. A part of Mac worried. He was hanging out with most of his co-workers who, around town, were known alcoholics. She'd sensed a gradual change in his attitude, a shift in the way he respected boundaries.

"Isn't that right, Mac?" Everyone in the group looked to her for an answer. "Mac?" Georgia waved a hand in front of Mac's face. "Earth to Mac?" A few people snickered. "She's drunk already."

"No," Mac half-responded. Everyone continued to stare at her. "I mean...yes? Yes. That's exactly it." All she wanted to do was go to bed. Couldn't they see that? Didn't they know? Heath raised his hand and hovered it near her, choosing to settle it on the top of her knee. She grimaced while flicking it off and hoping that no one noticed or asked questions.

The satisfied group returned to their laughter and conversation. The lack of wind had allowed Heath to have a few of his new friends over to sit around a fire with a few drinks. Mac insisted on inviting Georgia. Everyone talked and joked deep into the evening. After what Mac considered an excessive amount of time, one by one, the guests retreated to their trailers until only Mac and Heath remained.

He lounged back in his chair and swopped his arm around Mac's shoulders. "Do you mind getting' me 'nother?"

She lectured him before standing. "You've had enough."

A few seconds passed. Heath stood as well. "One more?"

"You don't need any more, Heath." She huffed, "It's those guys at work. They've changed you...you're not like you used to be at all. You're smoking more, being belligerent...all you do is drink and—"

"Maybe 'cause that's all there is to do," he scoffed.

Mac ignored him and threw a couple buckets of dirt over the fire and followed him into their trailer. She took a quick glance around, as she always did when entering, her attempt to remind herself that, indeed, it was her life, her option, her only choice. The dilapidated space was all she had and at first the atmosphere disgusted Mac. The fixtures and flooring were older than her dad's trailer, but with consistent work from her and Heath, they'd managed to update it.

"I'm going to bed." Heath interrupted her attempt to turn by positioning his arms around her. "Heath, I mean it. I'm tired." She tried to pull them away.

"I'm going to bed with ya," he slurred and moved closer to her.

"No, you have the couch. That was part of our deal, remember?"

His arms wrapped tighter around her and slid below her hips and back up. The bitter smell of alcohol from his breath caused her to fight the urge to gag. "It's been weeks. How much longer you gonna make me wait?"

Heath leaned closer to go in for a kiss, but his face met the palm of Mac's hand, and the impact sobered him up. Before he could respond, Mac escaped out the still-open door, leaving her regretful husband behind.

Fifteen

Since agreeing to give Heath a chance, Mac fought the urge to visit Bridgette as though it was a dark plague that refused remove its claws from her. The dreams would have to be enough, she reminded herself many times. She recalled Heath's snake-like hands as they slithered down her hips, gripping and constricting her. Every choice she had made threatened to siphon the life from her. She was done, and if the Bridgette across the bridge was to be the death of her, all the better.

The wind remained calm, and a grateful Mac made a quick job of running to the thick fence of briars and bushes and fighting her way through them. She'd grown attuned to the relentless barrier and could locate openings with ease. She moved deeper through the forest, and all the while she wondered if Bridgette would be there, somehow.

Why would she? After all, Mac had fled from her, rejected her. Mac pushed through the brambles that scratched their way up her bare legs until she arrived at the bank of the alluring creek.

The water ran and trickled in a soothing cadence of bells. Mac closed her eyes and took a deep breath in. She thanked the moment as it stretched as long as the creek itself, never seeming to have an end. "Maybe moments don't have ends. Maybe a single moment can last as long as I would like it to," she said.

She broke from her serenity to inspect up and down the bank; no sign of Bridgette. Of course, there wouldn't be. The fact only made sense. The bubbling creek continued to speak to her in a soft whisper, as though it had a story to tell.

"I'm not listening to you," she said between clenched teeth. "I can't anymore. It's over." She sighed. "I guess. It's all over." She turned to leave, figuring she'd return to the trailer, maybe talk to Heath.

Maybe she wanted too much; maybe happiness wasn't for her. What if being content was the most she should be asking for? She started for the bushes but as she did a shiver prompted her to look back. Bridgette stood in silence, and upon seeing her, Mac found that she couldn't cross the bridge quick enough.

Once on the other side, she grabbed her. "I'm so sorry." Her lips quivered and when Bridgette returned her hug, the girls sobbed.

Bridgette's tears rubbed off on Mac's cheek. "I know. I know you are." After a while, Bridgette pulled back. "Come, to the field. The moon is bright."

The girls held hands in a tight grip and walked to the field where they both sat on the brittle grass. Bridgette leaned into Mac who wrapped her arms around her in response. "There's nothing to do now," Mac whispered. "I married him. There's no way to get unmarried. I'll run away with you tonight, but to do so will make me wanted in every village we could escape to. The news will travel."

A long silence. "Unless..."

"Unless what?"

Bridgette's chilly fingers walked their way up Mac's neck. "Unless you became a—no, I can't say it."

Mac turned to her and brushed a curl from her face. "Say what?"

"I can't even suggest it." She looked away.

Mac coaxed the girl's face back to meet her own. "If it's an option, please, suggest it."

After a pause, Bridgette spoke. "Unless you become a widow."

Mac thought for a while. "But that means..."

"Heath would have to die," Bridgette finished with the hint of a smile.

A dry breeze ran through the field, and Mac shivered as the thought of betrayal coursed through her. Could she do that, *kill* somebody? Her best friend, even? The short answer was no. Even after how he'd been acting, there was no way she could steal the life of another human being in exchange for her own happiness.

"We have to think of another way." She shivered. "I can't do that."

"You can't *not* do it. Are you telling me you can seriously force yourself to be happy with him for the rest of your life when it's only been a few weeks and you're running back to me?"

"Yes, I can tell you that. I can't kill someone else. I can't do that. Not for you, not for me."

Bridgette's stare was its own form of hypnosis when she looked Mac in the eyes. "Listen, I'm not going to be your side girl forever. I could meet someone else, take off, and then I'd stop waiting for you." She lowered her voice until it became a whisper. "Do this and your every desire will be waiting when you're finished."

"It's selfish of you to ask me to kill Heath."

"It's selfish of *you* to want me to hold on to hope that we can be together."

Mac sighed, and the grass crunched beneath the weight of her body when she fell back on it. Bridgette copied her and rested her head on Mac's chest. Mac studied the stars as they lit up the night sky. "How would I even do something like that?"

"Easy. Poison, push him down a flight of stairs, or over a bannister. Do you not have stairs?"

Bridgette's nonchalant answer frightened Mac, but she replied anyway. "I live in a trailer. You know that."

"Then how are you going to do it? It has to look like an accident."

"Well, no shit." She pressed her eyes shut. How did she go from never wanting to kill anyone to answering Bridgette's questions? She recovered her thoughts. "And who says I will do it, anyhow?"

"Hey..." Bridgette used the back of her hand to caress Mac's cheek with a gentleness she was sure she had never felt before. Mac wondered how someone capable of such tenderness could fathom a plan so sinister as to include murder.

"I just...it's just that I don't think I can do something like this. It's, uh, I don't even know."

Bridgette whispered in her ear. "You don't have to know, because what you *do* know is what we have together. You know how you feel when you're around me, how happy you can be, Mac." Her words swirled through the night air and a sense of eerie peace filled Mac's body.

Mac released a pent-up breath.

"Be happy with me." Bridgette smoothed Mac's hair behind her ear. "*Mackenzie...*" her soft whisper was as chilling as it was exhilarating. For a moment, Mac felt like she actually *could* kill Heath. Bridgette continued in a low tone. "In the morning you'll leave, and we'll be together again when the deed is done. We can start our life, together. And you, my dear, will never have to worry about anything again. It will be as though we rule the world."

Sixteen

"Mac, I do love you. I've come to truly love you. It's the one thing that scares her. She's going to use it to manipulate you." The warm apparition stood in front of Mac beneath the moonlight in the same field she'd fell asleep in with Bridgette.

"You know I love you, too."

"But she's not me. Banish her and free me. Someday our souls can be together. If not, she will drain you until there is nothing left."

"I can't stay away from her."

"Mac, why not?"

"She's you."

Mac awoke in her familiar bedroom and double-checked the surroundings. The dreams were becoming too real, too ominous and threatening. Maybe once her and Bridgette could finally be together, they'd stop.

Thoughts of their conversation spun in her mind. How *could* they be together? Heath would have to die, but she'd decided she wouldn't be the one to kill him. Mac pulled the photograph from inside her pillow case and studied it. Desire overcame her like a curse of death. Everything she thought she ever wanted existed within the bottomless blue eyes that belonged to Bridgette Dawning, and despite the black and white newspaper picture, she could almost make out their color.

Heath never bothered to ask where Mac ran off to, but she had a feeling he already knew she'd been to Devil's Creek. After what he did, he wouldn't bother negating her actions. The only interaction between them was awkward at best, and he hadn't said a word to her since that evening.

Every time she thought about the way he touched her that night, his breath, his hands running down her hips, she fumed. And, for a moment, that anger served as a reminder of her conversation with Bridgette. The memory stirred through her mind and mixed with recollections of Bridgette's soft whispers when they'd spoke in Paradise Grove.

Even then, the recollection of that night came riddled with warnings from the version of Bridgette that visited Mac in her dreams. Fear that someone as gentle as Bridgette could persuade her to end someone's life invaded her thoughts. She knew she'd never stepped back to make sense of the situation. She was too far gone, swept away by the fantasy, intrigued by how a dead girl could feel so real in life and in her dreams.

Was Bridgette somehow split in two when she died? If so, how could that be? The only thing Mac knew for sure was that she loved the girl. She'd do anything, but could she bring herself to carry out the cruel plan?

She took a few steps into the kitchen and grabbed a frying pan and turned the stove on. From the refrigerator, she pulled a carton of eggs and a pad of butter. As the butter sizzled against the heated pan, she sorted through her thoughts.

Could she do it, kill him? Could she, really?

Mackenzie... A whisper breezed around her body and she shuddered.

"Who's there?" She looked from one side to the other. "Of course, no one's here." She told herself. "Stupid..." she shook her head and checked on the eggs.

Mackenzie...

She turned around again. "Georgia?" She peeked around the corner. If anyone would've came in, she'd have heard the door open. "I'm losing my mind..."

All your desires...

"Is this a joke?" The voice was directly behind her, but each time she looked, no one was around.

Everything you could ever want...

"Bridgette?"

Kill him...

"I'm giving you one chance to show yourself." She held the spatula up as though it would protect her from what she couldn't see.

Kill him...

"Stop!" She ran her hands through her hair. "Just Stop!"

Kill...

"No!" she fired back. She was well-aware of the word "kill" spiraling through her being but was determined to let nothing sway her conscious choice. "Leave!"

A maniacal laugh preceded another demand. *Kill...*

"I will not!" She turned from the stove to yell into a shadow of nothing. "No!"

Now.

Her body seemed to absorb the word. She couldn't let it go. It wouldn't let go of her.

"Kill him, now," she whispered to herself. The solution had never been as clear; it all began to make sense in her mind. He really did need to die.

The eggs sizzled until they burned in the pan. Even when the door opened and slammed right behind her, Mac was motionless.

Without warning Heath approached her from behind, his body making a slow rocking motion against hers. He didn't bother to ask, no consent, just like that. "I think it's time." He blew the words into her ear. "Don't you?"

The voice continued. *Does he think he owns you, maybe?*

One of his hands slid up her shirt. "Mac?"

"Back off," she muttered, although she couldn't figure out who she was talking to.

His hand continued exploring her warm skin and his lips met the side of her neck. "Baby—"

Heath didn't have a chance to finish. Mac spun around, and in one quick snap, the heated bottom of the cast-iron skillet howled against his temple, and charcoaled pieces of egg went flying. He didn't even have the opportunity to be stunned; a few more slams into his head, and his lifeless body stumbled once and smacked against the wall before slumping into a heap of the human being he'd once been.

As if coming out of a temporary spell, Mac's head spun with guilt—regret, hurt, anger filled her until she found herself unable to move. What had she done? She recalled the increasing vividness of her dreams, the voices and whispers. For whom or what had she done it?

"Heath?" She ran to him and shook the still body. "Oh my God! What did I do?" She looked around her. "What did *you* do?" She turned back to Heath. "Heath?" How would she explain to the police that it wasn't her? How would she get them to believe her? "There's no way. They'll put me in jail. They'll blame me, and I didn't do it. That wasn't me," she said aloud.

Without thinking to pack, she grabbed a small bit of cash and fled. She ran past row after row of trailers, past her dad's trailer. All the while, she fought the clouds of thick dust and the sharp wind. With each step she took the ground felt as though it was spinning beneath her feet. It threatened to bottom out at any time. In her mind, she was falling. To where, though? Straight to hell? To darkness?

She stopped at the thistle-barrier that separated the community from the evil of Devil's Creek. "What have you done, Mac?" She spun in a half circle and screamed into the wind and dirt. "What have you *done?*"

Where were the voices? The whispers and shadows that haunted her being? She didn't have to fight through the barrier that time. It had opened, wide, welcoming her. More thoughts intruded her mind. If she disappeared, Heath wouldn't be discovered for how many days? Two? Three? Would they believe someone broke in and killed him? Maybe they'd believe she was kidnapped.

"Where are you?" she huffed. "Where are you *now?*" No response. "Coward!"

When Mac reached the creek, she didn't bother to search for Bridgette. A part of her didn't even want to see the girl. All she wanted to do was run, to escape. Instead of pausing, she ran straight across the wooden bridge that would lead her through the outskirts of Paradise Grove to Towne Greene.

Seventeen

The afternoon sun didn't affect the dimly lit parsonage where the nervous shell of a being replaced a once confident man. Torn pages of the Bible plastered the walls, covering stained-glass depictions of the Virgin Mary holding baby Jesus and Noah welcoming animals aboard the faith-built ark. Page after page lined the wooden floor.

"Just leave me alone!" he screeched into nothingness. Silence drummed through the room. "Where?" He jumped from his seat and walked around the desk. "Where are you now?" He laughed out loud and shook his fist at a scene of the rock rolled away from Jesus' empty tomb. "Where are you now?"

The door startled Colstock and a few pages scattered as it flung open and shut with the same rapid motion. A frantic Samuel Johnson stood in the foyer. He surveyed the room. "What of this?" He motioned to the pages of the Bible that were strewn around him. "Never mind. There's no time. Come. A matter of the utmost importance is upon us." While he moved toward Colstock, he took care to avoid stepping on the sacred pages.

Colstock straightened himself and smoothed his unruly hair. "What matter?"

"A girl, from across the creek." He caught his breath. "A hunter has witnessed her, in Paradise Grove. All the town is gathering on the top of the hill. If you do not address this, chaos will ensue."

Without further hesitation, the Pastor gathered himself and followed Samuel out the door and to the meadow of grass that spread just before the incline. "You are sure she's from the other side?" The men continued with haste.

"Certain. This rumor is not false." Samuel turned to Colstock who came to a halt. "This matter, it could be our freedom."

Colstock narrowed his eyes. "Freedom? I'm afraid I don't quite understand."

"Yes, it could be our opportunity to express truth." Samuel brushed some dirt from the pastor's shoulder. "Perhaps, Elijah, perhaps it is time."

Colstock's expression hardened. "The truth would be...it would be my destruction, my demise. The truth is shame."

"Shame?" Samuel gasped, unable to believe what he had heard. "Colstock, my dear."

"Speak no more of this. The truth cannot, *will not*, be revealed."

Samuel's nose flared from the hurt he tried to process but couldn't. "Then whatever lies, whatever destruction, you will bring it all upon yourself."

The two continued up the hill without saying anything more. Clouds filled the sky and threatened the people of the town with the rain that seemed to never come, the rain that had compromised their crops and their once picturesque land.

All around Colstock, citizens were gathering at the top of the hill. If what Samuel said was true, the entirety of Paradise Grove could be contaminated with The Sickness. If the girl from the other side of the creek spoke, no one would be safe. That much became a nervous realization that infected his consciousness. She, too, would need to be destroyed.

Eighteen

Mac froze in front of the Paradise Grove hunter and the crowd that formed a circle around her. She conducted a frantic search for Bridgette. Nothing. She studied her surroundings; behind her stood an abrupt cliff, to her sides, people, and in front of her, even more people.

The hunter made slow circles around her, studying her carefully. "No water." He felt the ends of her short hair. "Not one drop. What witchcraft did you use to cross the creek without getting wet? What devil are you?"

"I crossed the bridge." The man cocked his head, but Mac insisted, "There was...a bridge that connected our side with Paradise Grove."

"There would not be a bridge. Never," he countered. "We would not connect ourselves to such an evil."

In that moment, Mac realized she'd been abandoned. All the promises that Bridgette made to her about her every desire manifesting seemed to wither like the dry grass below her feet. She imagined herself meeting the same fate as Bridgette, becoming the Paradise Grove spectacle.

"You entered the water. You must have." As he accused her, the crowd closed in, but when they neared her, she found an opening and fled farther up the hill. If she could just reach the other side, she'd be able to disappear into the forest and maybe they would lose her trail.

She looked back to see she had outrun the hunter and the crowd with ease. She couldn't stop, though. She had to keep going, but when she turned to speed up, Bridgette stood in front of her, arms spread wide. "Oh my God, you made it."

"He's dead. Heath is dead." Mac fell into Bridgette's ice-cold arms. "What have I done?"

Bridgette answered with a question of her own. "Who's behind you?"

"A hunter spotted me. The entire town, they're coming. We have to get down the hill, to the woods."

Bridgette's calm disposition didn't waver. "It's okay. It's going to be okay."

"Bridgette, we need to run." But she didn't move. "Bridgette?"

"There's people approaching you from the other side of the hill. You're surrounded now. There's nowhere to go," the hunter warned.

Bridgette stood in front of Mac. "Stay close to me."

A light thunder rumbled through the sky as it darkened above them. The crowd closed in on the girls, and Bridgette took Mac's hand.

The only option Mac thought she had was trusting Bridgette's guidance. "Where are we going?"

"Closer to the edge."

"The edge?"

But Bridgette didn't stop to answer more questions. The hunter was nearing them. Mac looked down into the shining water and took several steps from the drop-off.

"All the town is upon us," the hunter said. "Johnson has gone to fetch our pastor, Reverend Colstock. Only he will Divine what will come of you, girl."

Mac's body shook as a crowd approached the scene. "And what of her?" She motioned to Bridgette.

"Her?"

"Yeah, her." She pulled Bridgette closer. "Can she be saved?"

The hunter grimaced. "Are you delusion, girl?"

Mac looked to Bridgette and then to her adversary. "She's right here."

"Reverend Colstock will deal with you and your devilish illusion," he scoffed.

Bridgette looked to Mac. "Don't listen to him. He's just trying to trick you."

As the crowd neared them, they formed a half-circle around Mac and Bridgette. Some people prayed, some fell to their knees in penance, others mocked and scorned Mac. The spectacle continued until Colstock, along with Samuel Johnson, approached and made his way to the circle.

"Spare her. Do what you must with me," Mac pleaded.

Colstock studied Mac. "Her?"

"Bridgette, Bridgette Dawning. She's here. Can't you see her?"

But when Mac turned, Bridgette wasn't there. It was only her and the edge of the cliff. A thick, ominous cloud swirled where Bridgette once stood. *Colstock...*

Pastor Colstock's eyes widened. He lifted an accusatory finger to Mac. "It's her. The Sickness is in her, next to her. See it with your eyes." He panned to the shadow. "*This!*"

The curious crowd took a few steps back in attempts to keep themselves safe from catching the disease.

Mac stared at the unmoving, dark spot of air. "I-I..." She waved her hand through it. "Bridgette?"

"No, Mac." An illuminated, angelic version of Bridgette covered head to toe in a near blinding light stood in front of her. "Mac." She extended a hand. "Come to me."

One slow step after another, Mac walked to Bridgette.

No! Don't listen, Mac... A cold hiss sounded from behind her.

Mac recognized the voice from the trailer, from when she—Mac blinked hard and swallowed—killed Heath. The whisper seemed to pull her backwards, toward the darkness. "No." She struggled against the shadowed temptation.

Mackenzie...

None of the curious Paradise Grove onlookers moved. Most were fixed on the near blinding illumination in front of them that increased in brightness as she spoke. "For over one hundred years the Colstock family has deceived this town, and you would let Elijah Colstock continue to do so. Your neighbors, the ones you banished across the way, they spoke of the screams of children coming from the woods. Were not those screams real? A century ago, did you not deny the safety of your children upon one man's word that the evil was that of a demon? And what now? You would kill her. You would put me to death to protect more lies? It is not who you love that is the source of evil. It is the collective unwillingness to acknowledge truth."

"Lies!" Colstock wiped more sweat as it ran down his brow. A fly buzzed around him. "Be gone with you!" he yelled into the air.

Before the apparition could speak again, a thick cloud of dark fog confronted her. *Speak not of this,* it hissed, *lest your soul be at risk.*

Upon the threat against who Mac had determined was the true spirit of Bridgette Dawning, she took off toward the darkness. She moved between the golden light and the shadowy haze that was ready to snuff out the brightness. Mac looked to the crowd and fixed her eyes on Reverend Elijah Colstock. In that single moment, everything she'd seen in her dreams made sense.

"All your lies. That is what has brought this on. You lied to the community about your love for Samuel to protect your notoriety. You lied to Samuel. Your feelings were never forbidden...because of you the truth was, though." She thought back to what she'd seen from behind the tree. "You, trying to cover up your affections for Samuel Johnson, your fear of losing notoriety." Her head panned the crowd. "Can't you see it now?" Colstock's eyes widened. "Can't you see it? You created your own demon."

Your soul shall I take... The darkness began to advance on Bridgette, but as hard as it tried to overtake the girl, Mac pushed back with even more willpower. It was as though her hand was enough to fend the blackened swarm away from the light.

Mac looked up, in brevity, and locked eyes with Colstock whose pale face was drenched in sweat. Flies buzzed around him in droves. "Your lies might have taken her life, but they will not have her soul." She gave the darkness one final, large shove backwards but was too busy focusing on the pastor to watch her footing.

As the evil plummeted from the cliff toward the rocky bottom of Devil's Creek, so did Mac. Thick silence replaced the hilltop where darkness once stood, save for drums of thunder from the clouds above. Tedious moments passed; no one dared do little more than take a shallow breath here and there, as should be the case when over a century of lies have been unveiled. The only movement appeared in drops of rain that fell, one after the other, from relieved clouds.

Conclusion

The rain didn't stop. It was as if it couldn't even if it wanted to. The never-ending waters flooded basements which ended up overflowing to first floors, creating unlivable homes. Failed attempts to build temporary shelters on the top of the hill left residents with nowhere to go. The swamped homes created mudslides down the hill and into the already overfilled Devil's Creek. Citizens of Paradise Grove found themselves left with no other choice than to seek the help of their contaminated neighbors.

The reunion wasn't without its share of aggression and hesitation. After a century of being non-existent, why should the once arid side of the creek allow its oppressors any type of refuge? Some protested the integration, but eventually Paradise Grove won out and the other town allowed the flooded citizens across Devil's Creek.

Between the raging creek and sliding mud, residents of Paradise Grove fought for their lives, and many of them ended up losing the battle before they were able to cross the creek to safety. Some refused to move, still insisting the creek was contaminated and anyone touching its waters, accidental or not, was consenting to sin. Those were the ones who stayed behind, fighting for their idea of Paradise Grove, and dying along with their definitions of what it meant to be holy and righteous, drowning in a deluge of lies they chose to hold on to.

Weeks passed. The seemingly infinite depth of sand continued to absorb the rain. Just like with any time of renewal, when the storms ended, the once desert terrain saw new plant growth, and Paradise Grove drowned, along with its legacy of deceptions, in the same waters it once claimed to be the source of The Sickness.

Upon hearing tales of his daughter's demise, Howell scoffed. "All these years, all you all believed was that by keeping us penned up over here like a bunch of livestock, you were safe from this Sickness. Turns out, maybe after all this time, it was our lives that were saved."

Investigative services from Towne Greene arrived soon after the rains stopped to check into Heath's death. During the accident reconstruction, they ruled it a homicide. The dilemma being, how could a girl of five feet, five inches who wasn't said to be muscular hit a boy as large as Heath with enough force to nearly kill him on impact. She had to have had help, they insisted, because, to them, no girl could accomplish the act alone.

Was it because of adultery? Self-defense on Mac's part? Despite whispers in the town and admissions in interviews that talked of Mac's late-night escapades in the woods, no one could give specific names. When two or three residents mentioned Bridgette Dawning, detectives looked into it just to find that she'd died before Heath of "unknown causes".

They interviewed Mac's only friend, Georgia, but couldn't find enough evidence to say conclusively that she was the accomplice. Infuriated and shamed by the accusations, Georgia eventually moved to Towne Greene. Acting never quite worked out for her as no one from Towne Greene was willing to hire a girl from the Paradise Grove settlement. She spent years working as a waitress before settling down with an accountant and giving birth to twins. Those who knew of how the sunlight was said to weave through her hair and the sky to sparkle in her eyes would later claim that over the decades, they faded into unrecognizable dull shells of the light they once carried.

Heath's parents were never able to forgive Howell, even though no one was able to prove Mac was the reason behind the death of their only son. Needing to hold someone responsible, they maintained their grudge throughout the years, causing a rift to tremor through the city.

Howell never abandoned his search for the truth of what happened to Mac. He reviewed files compiled by Towne Greene detectives and traveled from witness to witness to gather his own accounts. The most accurate was Samuel Johnson, who citizens never rendered complicit in the unnecessary murder of Bridgette Dawning. Samuel offered that he was standing near the edge of the cliff, ready to jump out of sorrow. He recalled that when Mac stumbled off the ledge, the cloud of darkness that went with her coupled with the onset of heavy rain made visibility impossible. In fact, no one could say with certainty that Mac fell to the creek. Howell never found the body of his daughter.

What of Samuel Johnson? Just as the town was destroyed by floods of truth, he too was left with no more than memories of the person he considered to be the love of his life. Even then, he questioned if what he and Colstock shared was love. Despite a few attempts by Leonard Torrelson to become close to him, Samuel spent the remainder of his life in a cabin nestled deep in the forest.

The most gruesome of accounts, however, surrounded Elijah Colstock, who witnesses claimed shortly after Mac fell from the ledge, found himself face to face with a grizzly apparition of Lady Withermoore. They said her wide eyes opened into a ghastly grin and the only words from her mouth were, "*Lies...*" and that with one point of a shaking finger, she sucked what was left of Reverend Colstock into nothing more than a shriveled shell covered in droves of hungry flies. When a few brave citizens dared to return to the site, the flies had vanished and Colstock's body was never recovered.

More often than not, when faced with the truth, it was easier to speak of fables and lies. Residents held tight to the belief that by deflecting what was real, perhaps one also deflected the culpability that seemed to linger for decades before dying. As much effort as citizens invested into denying the memories of Bridgette Dawning and Mackenzie Howell, the lovers who were separated by death, and who, in the minds of a few, had no business falling in love in the first place, as Bridgette was not actually alive, the stories remained not to be forgotten. For, the truest of claims often stemmed from whispers that were told around evening campfires between couples who sat in a lush field of thick grass—that on a full moon, the freed spirits of Mackenzie and Bridgette appeared, wrapped in shrouds of blinding light, laughing, chasing, and holding one another—on the forbidden ground that kissed the edge of Devil's Creek.

The End

About the Author

Erin Crocker was born in Kansas City, Missouri. Later, she moved to southern Missouri and eventually wound up in Fredericksburg, Virginia.

She holds an A.A.S in General Studies with an emphasis in Police Science and a Certificate of Education from Germanna Community College and a Bachelor's of English, Linguistics, and Communications from the University of Mary Washington.

Throughout her writing career, Erin's short fiction and flash fiction pieces have won national and international literature competitions.

Erin also works as an assistant editor for Salem, Massachusetts based FunDead Publications and participates on various literary and author panels in addition to sitting as a judge in writing competitions.

In her spare time, Erin enjoys delightful activities that include playing the stock market, studying cryptocurrency, analyzing philosophy, and watching documentaries.

Made in the USA
Middletown, DE
23 October 2021